ONCE UP
... IN FINSBURY

ONCE UPON A TIME
in FINSBURY

L A PERDONI

Sunflower sketches by Andrea Chappell

First published in 2021 by L A Perdoni

lapatph19@gmail.com

Text copyright © L A Perdoni 2021
Cover and title page illustrations copyright © Doug H 2021
Flower illustrations copyright © Andrea Chappell

ISBN: 978-1-9162821-1-7

A CIP record for this book is available from the British Library

Typeset by The Holywell Press, holywellpress.com
Printed in Great Britain by The Holywell Press, Ltd., Oxford

'Once upon a time … in Finsbury'

'ONCE UPON A TIME...'

Giuseppina Bussetta

- One -

The landmark of the village was the church, with its delicate spire that rose above the ridged red roof tiles of the houses, a white triangle reflecting the sunlight, pointing into the often brilliant blue of the Northern Italian sky and reminding visitors and residents alike of the trinity worshipped within.

The interior of the little church was simple in its design. Everything was made of wood from the roof beams to the pews, the beams gleaming with painted decoration that was regularly refreshed, the pews gleaming with the beeswax lavished upon them regularly by the faithful women of the community.

A gallery provided an upper floor around three-quarters of the church and this was supported by simple wooden columns near most of which stood old carved statues of saints and angels with their candle-stands beside them. Along one side of the church were the two confessional boxes and by the column next to them stood the pride and joy of the church's collection of statuary, a vivacious Madonna holding out to the world an infant with arms outstretched in welcome and the sweetest smile of understanding and perception that one could hope to see in a time of distress.

The candle-stand before the Madonna was always full and the light from the tapers flickered against the stars of silver and gold that dotted the Virgin's mantle.

Giuseppina Bussetta, known to her friends and relatives as Pina, was a regular daytime visitor to the church and enjoyed her duties as a cleaner. She saved her attentions to the candle-stand to the end of the jobs and once the spilled wax had been scraped away and the blue kneeling pad on the priedieu had been plumped up, she allowed herself the luxury of a few moments before the statue of the Madonna.

In an empty church these few moments were often spent in a monologue conducted out loud with Pina providing what she imagined might be the answers to her questions along lines similar to these:

'So, you think I should go to Lugagnano on Friday rather than Wednesday then? Well, I'm sure you're right because I can see Maria then and give her the salami.'

'So, it would be better to keep quiet about Donatella's husband and the goat? You're right, if I say what I saw, the children will suffer but then he needs taking down a peg or two. *Eh bene*, I'll leave that to you...'

And so on...

But a constant theme of her thoughts voiced out loud was her own unmarried status. Pina was neither young nor old. She had not always lived in the village though she had been born there. For a few years she had gone to live in London with her sister, Lola, and had trained there as a school teacher for the very young. But when her parents had become frail and not really able to look after themselves, she, as the unmarried daughter, had returned to take care of them in the village.

Her departure from London had been sudden and there were many unkind tongues only too ready to speculate on the 'real' reason for her departure. A postcard sent to a friend from Belgium while she was en route back to the village only spawned further rumours, especially as the picture was of a convent.

But Pina devoted herself to looking after her old people while they were alive as she had been their last child, born when they were quite old, and now in her early 30s her self-sacrifice was showing its downside. Her parents were both dead. One of her sisters had emigrated to Australia and was rarely heard of, and the other lived in London with her daughters. By common consent, Pina had inherited the house and a comfortable income but now she was all alone. She was not unattractive even if life in a village did not allow her the refinements of regular visits to hairdresser and beautician which those living in a town might enjoy. Her hair retained its natural colour and sheen, her complexion was fresh and her eyes bright and lively.

As she was a trained teacher of younger children, for many years she had taken charge of the local school. But her parents' increasing infirmity and the evacuation of villages for towns by most people with children over time had led to the disappearance of work and when the last of the youngsters had left, the school was closed. So here she was, alone, and with little hope of meeting a husband unless she too closed up her family home and moved to town. But who would want to buy her out? No one was really interested in an old fashioned house in a fairly remote village.

And so, with such thoughts repeatedly running through her mind, she would usually conclude her prayers by asking, '*Eh bene*, Madonnina, are you going to send me a husband?'

The smile on the Madonna's face always seemed enigmatic.

It was a fairly ordinary day in May, one of those when the rota demanded Pina's undivided attention to the pews with her beeswax polish. She had concluded all her other tasks and was ready to turn her attention to her favourite cleaning pursuit when she realised that her basket of materials was lacking the tub of beeswax. She recalled instantly that she had finished the old one the last time she was there and should have replaced the old container with a new one before leaving home. It had just slipped her mind.

The morning was fresh but there was no one about so she saw no harm in returning home without locking the church behind her. She would not be long.

It so happened that the parish priest was looking out of his window just after Pina had left. He failed to see her but he did notice that church door was unusually ajar and went over to investigate. On entering the church he saw the cleaning materials in the pews and realised what had happened but before he could return home, he heard voices in conversation, well in fact it was just one voice, but it was easy to mistake the monologue for conversation. Feeling embarrassed as if he had been caught out eavesdropping, and also not wishing to be drawn into any lengthy conversation himself with his well-intentioned but very chatty parishioners, without thinking, he darted into the darkness of a confessional box and remained there quietly. He had not bargained for Pina's relentless monologue and when eventually she stopped her earnest polishing and settled on the priedieu, he was astonished to hear her ask her conventional question.

'Are you going to send me a husband, Madonnina?' And without thinking what he was doing, he found himself whispering, 'No.'

For a moment there was a pause, and then Pina asked again and again the priest replied, 'No!' with the open Italian vowel sound echoing from the recesses of the box.

The priest was aware of Pina getting to her feet.

'*Eh, bene,*' she said out loud, '*Taci, bambino, lascia parlare la tua santa Madre!*' – Be quiet, child, and let your holy mother do the talking!

But this time wisdom prevailed, and discretion and the priest remained silent.

About a month later, Pina was engaged in her usual devoted polishing in the church and as usual, she finished on the kneeler before the Madonna.

She knelt with her head down for a moment and then started her usual question when she was suddenly startled and had to blink to make sure she was not seeing things as between the extended hands of the Holy Infant was an envelope, slightly curved to fit safely there without falling, and written on the envelope was her name: Giuseppina Bussetta.

With almost reverent care she took the envelope into her own hands and unsealed it.

The letter was written in English. The note paper's heading advised that it was from the church of Our Lady of Amwell, in the area of London known as Finsbury. It was from the parish priest and it was an invitation to her to return to London and take up a post looking after a widower and his young daughter, both Italian in origin. There was hardly any detail given, just an earnest entreaty to consider the request and reply as soon as possible.

Where had the letter come from? Clearly Padre Girolamo had had something to do with it but when asked, he feigned surprise, smiled and extended his hands in the particular way that clerics have of showing that things are not always within their sphere of influence.

A day or two later, a letter arrived from London via the more conventional postal service. This was from Pina's sister, Lola, urging her to shut up the house in the village and return to London as she was sorely missed especially by her nieces. Lola added the extra inducements that the shops were no longer subject to severe rationing and that the two old ladies who ran the Haberdashery on the left hand side going up Amwell Street had found a few extraordinary suppliers and her sister should come and see for herself what a treasure trove the shop was now.

Lola and her two daughters lived a little further out in Islington, rather than in Finsbury, but these streets were all familiar to Pina and she loved them.

The encouragement from her sister and the mysterious letter from the parish priest of Our Lady of Amwell combined to make her reconsider her position and life in the village and so over the next month she set about putting the house to bed, ensuring that linens were safe from mould and moth, that glass and china was wrapped and stored with care. She knew that neighbours would keep an eye on things and on her last morning she delivered a spare set of keys to Secondina her best friend, and with just one large suitcase and an over shoulder-bag she walked down the slope towards the place where the *corriere* would pass. The church door was open and as she had time, she popped in and knelt before the Madonna. The enigmatic smile of both mother and infant warmed her for the adventure that lay ahead.

- Two -

The landmark of Amwell Street was the local pub, known as Dirty Dick's. This was situated almost at the top of the hill before the street passed into the curiosity that calls itself Claremont Square on its summit or led off to the right into Myddleton Square where what remained of an Anglican church still dominated the gardens.

The church of Our Lady of Amwell was a long way from the summit, buried down by a main thoroughfare but still remarkable in its own way by reason of its warmly painted Calvary that graced its front wall.

On entering the church you might have thought that you were in a meeting hall for Presbyterians or Quakers, so un-churchy was the architecture but the presence of statues, candles and confessional boxes together with the red sanctuary light with its comforting glow would soon dispel any doubts that you were in a Catholic church.

'So,' thought Pina, 'this is my new church.'

It was darker than she remembered it from years before because the wide display of glass on the side windows had all been painted with black-out paint and no one had as yet got round to removing the evidence of war-time. And there were new statues too. The one that particularly caught her eye was of her own patron saint, St Joseph, after whom she had been named Pina. Traditionally the saint is shown holding a lily but in this group the older man has his arm over the shoulder of a boy of about twelve years old. The startling feature of the group however was that Pina recognised the boy's face: it had the same features and smile of understanding and perception which had graced the infant in the Madonna's arms in the village church. This boy was that infant, grown up.

The Presbytery was only a door away from the entry to the church. Pina had phoned to make an appointment to see the parish priest as he had requested in his letter and at the appointed time she appeared on the doorstep. No sooner had she pressed the bell than the door opened and a smiling lady, slightly older than herself, welcomed her in.

'You must be Miss Bussetta,' she said. 'Do come in. Father Martyn is waiting for you in the sitting room.' The voice was soft and Irish. 'I won't be a moment. I have the kettle on already. So would you be after taking tea or coffee?'

'Brigid makes a lovely milky coffee,' said a voice from another room. 'I can recommend it.'

'But I know you I-talians love your real coffee so I must warn you I only do Nescaff. The proper stuff's too strong for the tastes in this house. But I'll do it with hot milk if you prefer it that way.'

'Don't go to any bother,' replied Pina, rather overwhelmed by the instant hospitality which would have matched anything offered in an Italian home. 'I'm very happy with tea.'

'Oh, good. That's a relief. I'm Brigid by the way. Come on through!'

And the front door was closed and the sitting room door opened. Pina found Fr Martyn with hand outstretched. 'Come in, come in and be at home, Miss Bussetta, I feel I know you already: we have a mutual friend, Natalia Robertson?'

'Oh yes, Natty's a great pal of mine,' Pina replied. 'I saw her just last week. We often go to the pictures together.'

'Yes, I know,' said Fr Martyn. 'I'm quite a regular visitor to Granville Street myself – I can't resist her husband's prawn cocktail, and she makes the best chips ever! I'm a slave to my stomach, I'm afraid, even though Brigid' – who appeared at that very moment with a tea tray – 'tries to keep me under control!'

'*Try* is the operative word,' said Brigid, setting down the tray. 'But with his parish ladies all vying to charm him with their baking, it's an uphill struggle! There now…that's everything. So I'll leave you to it.'

'Well, now, please, you don't need to go on my account,' said Pina.

'Are you sure?' said the priest. 'Of course I'm happy for Brigid to hear anything I have to tell you. She knows it all already. We have no secrets from each other, except those of the confessional. It's best that way. I trust her totally and if she has to deal with anyone when I'm not here, she has a pretty good idea of how to sift the important from the trivial, and she deals with everyone with absolute kindness.'

'Oh Father, you'll be making me blush,' said the housekeeper. 'But it's true that it helps me a lot to understand.'

'And it helps me a lot to have a woman's perspective and to have someone to talk over things outside of my bachelor experience,' said the priest. 'But more of that later. Fetch yourself a cup, Brigid, and let's enjoy our tea and Brigid's lemon cake first.'

Which is exactly what they did, allowing Pina to settle into their convivial company more comfortably.

'So, now to the business in hand,' said Fr Martyn.

'I have an Italian parishioner living and working just a stone's throw from the church. He has a daughter of some eight years who goes to the Convent school in Duncan Terrace. He makes statues – in wood when there's a commission – but generally in plaster, though he carves the wood models from which the moulds are made himself. Most of his house is a factory. He lives there alone with the child and is worried that she is not being looked after properly. She has no mother.'

'So he's a widower, then?' asked Pina.

'Well…' said the priest.

'Well nothing…' interrupted Brigid. 'Tell it as it is, or shall I?'

'Go ahead,' said Fr Martyn. 'But this is for your ears only, Miss Bussetta.'

'Please call me Pina. It's easier.'

'He has a wife,' said Brigid, straight to the point. 'But she lives in Italy. The child thinks her mother is dead.'

'But why?'

'Because she's hospitalised…well, she's in a home, I don't know what they'd call it, a hospital maybe, for the mentally ill,' said Brigid. 'She suffered soon after the child was born and doctors can't do much for her state of mind. He told us there's no hope of her getting better. It's a private place. He visits when he can but there's little point. Signor Romani was intending to come over here anyway as he'd already bought the statue business. He left the child with the nuns to start with but then couldn't bear to be without her so brought her over and she's grown up here.'

'Poor man,' said Pina, 'But what can I do to help?'

Fr Martyn replied, 'Just be there as much as you can to deal with the practicalities. Shopping…cleaning…collecting from school…you know, everything that would relieve him and support him. He could certainly do with someone to look after the house. I know I do,' he added, glancing at Brigid.

Pina fell silent and clasped her hands on her lap.

'Tell me when the best time would be for me to pay him a visit,' she said.

'Thank you, Pina,' said Fr Martyn, leaning over from his chair and enclosing Pina's hands in his own. 'Thank you.'

- Three -

The sun was shining on the Saturday morning of that same week when Pina made her way to the neat street of houses within easy walking distance from where the church stood. She checked the number and took a moment before knocking. There were half shutters on the ground floor window and they were pulled back so that she could see into the front room partially from where she stood on the step. She was aware of an impression of colours in the room – red, brown, green and blue – and without peering too closely she was aware of racks with small figures arrayed on them. The basement area underneath this window was tidy but the shutters there were closed and revealed nothing to her gaze. The heavy knocker resounded on its base and the big front door opened a little. There in the doorway stood a child. A man's voice drifted down from somewhere in the heart of the house.

'Who is it, Chiara?'

'I'm Pina Bussetta and I've come to see Signor Romani. Would that be your daddy?'

'Pappa!' called back the child.

'Ask the lady in, Chiara,' said the voice.

And as Pina entered and closed the door behind her, the child ran along the hallway and up the stairs to where a man was just turning the bend. He was dressed in the brown overalls of a worker and the child ran under the embrace of his arm as he paused on the stair.

As the child turned to face Pina, the man rested his arm on her shoulder and a shaft of sunlight from the landing window lit up their faces.

With a glow of recognition, Pina saw on the child's face that sweet smile of understanding and perception with which she was so familiar.

'This is the lady who's come to look after us,' said Remo Romani as he squeezed his daughter's shoulders a little. 'Why don't you show her the way upstairs, Chiara, and make her feel at home?'

And obediently and enthusiastically, the child left her father's embrace and ran down towards Pina with arms outstretched.

'This way, this way,' she smiled.

Remo Romani

- One -

Pina was used to early rising. In the village she had always woken up as soon as it was light. She never drew the blinds or curtains as this early morning light invigorated her and she started her day with the dawn and started to wind down at dusk. So the regime imposed on her by her new responsibilities in London was no hardship at all, at least in the summer time, but on those dark northern winter mornings she had to set her alarm so as to be up and dressed and ready to walk from her sister's to the house of plaster saints in time to prepare Chiara for school and make breakfast for the child and her father as well as for herself. The arrangements worked well. She would walk Chiara to her convent school in Duncan Terrace, do a little shopping in Chapel market for their supper later in the day, return with it and prepare anything that was needed, and then on specific days would either clean the house or change the beds or take laundry to the baths in Merlin street. Whichever the tasks she had assigned to herself, she always made time to pop into Our Lady of Amwell church, if not for Mass then at least for a prayer and one of her regular meditations before the statue of the Madonna and sometimes in this church with her named patron saint, Joseph.

Remo made it his priority to collect his daughter from school in the afternoon as he had always done. Sometimes he would treat her to a short diversion on the way home via Lyons Tea Shop at the Angel where they might buy cakes for tea or perhaps a small bag of cellophane wrapped peppermint creams in white and pink and green, which they knew would please Pina. They often laughed at the little sweets with their pale reflection of the colours of the Italian flag and yet their totally English taste of sweetness and peppermint.

Sometimes the diversion would take them no further than the front of the old cinema which in its heyday had been a great Edwardian theatre, The Philharmonic, and Chiara would stare up at the statues and ask her father what the playbills posted outside said. Sometimes the short stop would be to see the blue kettle pumping out its steam into the street over the cafe that bore its name. This was always a treat and puzzlement. Just how did they get the steam to flow so constantly?

Pina would have the table set for tea ready for their arrival home and they ate together at about 5 p.m.

Chiara was made ready for bed and Pina would be off by about 6. Of course she had most of the afternoon free as well and none of her duties ever became onerous.

At weekends, the pattern changed and to start with she never went on Saturdays and Sundays at all. But as she became more integrated into the little family, there started to appear a sort of tangible gap between Friday night and Monday morning which all three didn't much like and so, almost without it being specified, Pina would have some reason to be at the house on a Saturday and once Chiara started her preparation for First Holy Communion, Pina would accompany father and daughter to Sunday Mass not at Our Lady of Amwell's but at St John's, the large church almost next door to the convent school in Duncan Terrace. This is where Franca, Pina's niece, had made her First Communion in the previous year. Franca's sister, Rosa, who was the same age as Chiara, would be making hers at the same time as Chiara this year.

- Two -

It was hard to believe that two years passed with this sort of pattern of life. Pina had time and opportunity to re-establish contact with her friends, especially her closest friend Natalia in Granville Street. Although the area was one of streets with no open spaces save for the gardens of the Squares, there was a strong feeling of living in a village community and Amwell Street itself had virtually all the shops anyone would need, with the two markets at its top and toe in Chapel Street and Exmouth Street that provided choice and variety, and the Italian quarter only a few streets away which filled the nostrils with the smells of home and the heart with a nostalgic yearning to be back in the hills under the blue skies where one belonged.

But that was always the question. Where did one belong? Pina would often talk about this with her sister, Lola, and Natty. All three had spent childhood days in Italy and yet here they were miles away in London, adapting to life in a city without a thought, except a nostalgic one, for the hills of Northern Italy. When they discussed the likelihood of returning there, a feeling almost of horror would sweep over them. How would they re-adapt to a world without a weekly visit to the cinema and a cosy evening in front of a T.V. screen, offering quiz shows and American comedy, and a chance to see how people lived in the rest of the world? It was unthinkable!

Not everyone was fortunate enough to own a television. Remo Romani had no intention of buying one and yet there were programmes especially aimed at children.

Sometimes Pina would take Chiara to tea at Natty's on a Sunday, with her nieces Franca and Rosa as well. Natty was always delighted to see them. Her husband made excellent cake so there was always something delicious for the children to eat and Pina's nieces made quite a friend of Chiara even though they went to different schools and they played happily together and enjoyed watching the Children's television with its News from Alexandra Palace and its little stories of Muffin the Mule and his friends.

The Sunday tea outings gave Remo a chance to spend time with his friends as well. He would meet them at the Club near St Peter's Church in Clerkenwell Road and have time to play cards and relax in male company as well as further his contacts and outlets for his work.

Such then was the pattern of Life.

- Three -

It was a Friday towards the end of the summer term in July when at the breakfast table, Remo suddenly cleared his throat.

'Pina, would you collect Chiara this afternoon from school, please?'

'Of course,' she replied, looking slightly puzzled. But it was not that unusual a request.

'And you needn't trouble with shopping for supper tonight. I'm going to cook, and I'll shop as well. I have a particular reason for doing so and I'll tell you both later today. So, Pina, the day's yours. I should've given you more notice, I know, so that you could plan it. I'm sorry about that.'

'Don't worry,' said Pina. 'Some of the mothers go for a coffee and a gossip at the Blue Kettle on a Friday and I'm usually too busy to join them, but it'll make a nice change for me today.'

Chiara hardly paid attention to this adult exchange even though what was about to happen would change her life forever.

The day passed very much as planned and when Pina and Chiara returned from school that afternoon, they found the table in the kitchen all set ready for a meal. There was just one small change which Chiara was quick to notice. Her napkin ring was in the wrong place. Usually Remo sat at the head of the table and Chiara and Pina on either side. The napkin ring that was Chiara's was set at the head of the table. It was nothing. A slip. Remo rarely set the table but when a little later they all gathered for the meal and Chiara made to rearrange the napkins, Remo said, 'No, cara. Today that is your place.' And he indicated his own chair with its side arms as his daughter's seat.

The element of surprise had clearly started. As they were eating in the kitchen, everything was ready to hand and they started with a great plate of prosciutto di Parma, cut so finely that you could see the light through it, with olives and a wonderfully fresh loaf that Remo had clearly made himself that day, open textured, slightly salty with a very black crust where it had caught in the oven.

Remo let them both enjoy as much as they wanted while he supervised the stirring of a pan of risotto ai funghi. There were three bowls of salad ready prepared on the side and when the riso was served steaming and the parmesan and black pepper had been sprinkled, Remo began.

'I can put you out of your misery,' he said. 'Pina, I have a question for you and Chiara, a decision for you to make, which is why today you're seated as mistress of the house.'

Both Pina and Chiara remained silent, and waited.

'Pina, will you move in here permanently? I'd very much like you to do that.'

Chiara hastily dropped her fork, clapped her hands over her head and exclaimed.

'Yes please, please, Pina, then I'll have a real mummy all the time.'

Pina's cheeks reddened and she didn't know where to focus her gaze. Her mind reacted swiftly. Several different shafts of thought criss-crossed. None of them found a place to settle: here was a chance to be part of a real family – the pleasure of being a mother and a wife – but no, not an actual mother and certainly not a wife. There was already a wife – in Italy. Or was Remo now a widower? He had never spoken of her to Pina. What she knew was only what Fr Martyn had told her at the start. Had that now changed? Each shaft of thought as swift as a lightning flash. And every one mistaken…

'And you, Chiara, your decision must come later and is to some extent dependent on Pina's reply. But I don't want any answers now. Just enjoy the riso and then we'll have our dessert. It's a bit wicked, but I've made zabaglione.'

It was a very good thing that there was so much food with such delicious tastes to indulge in and distract from the bomb-shelling of Remo's statements. When all was done, he told them to leave the dishes and kitchen for him to tidy later and to come and sit down as he had something to show them.

When all were comfortable, and coffee for himself and Pina was ready, Remo produced a letter.

'It's from Italy,' he began, 'and yes, you can have the stamps, cara!'

Again, Pina's heart rose to her throat. Surely he wasn't going to break the news about his wife's existence to Chiara only to tell her that she had died?

Nothing of the sort.

'I've been offered an amazing opportunity. A commission. To repair the 14 Stations of the Cross which were damaged by a bomb during the war – in wood.'

Pina allowed herself to breathe again.

Remo started to bubble with enthusiasm as he explained the details, so much so that he was almost unaware of his audience who sat quietly and let him expound without interruption.

'I knew about the job some time ago so I applied and submitted my designs, two of them in very full detail. I chose Jesus meeting the women of Jerusalem and the Deposition from the Cross. I'm sure it's my design for the first that's won me the invitation. You usually see Jesus with a crowd of women but I put in the foreground a woman with a young girl and I used you two as my models. Well, I thought, the Book says Jesus said 'Weep for yourselves and your children', so why not show the children or at least a representative of them as well? And with the Deposition, well, you'll see what I've done differently there when I show you the sketches. So, what do you think? Good news or good news?'

Pina had begun to piece together the unspoken parts during Remo's account and now she asked quietly.

'Does this mean you'll have to work in Italy?'

'Yes, didn't I say? It's for a more modern style new church being built in the North to replace a war damaged one. But they want to reuse as much of the damaged Stations from the old church as they can as a sort of continuation of tradition. I would have to be in Italy for quite a long time. I'd have a team of wood carvers to do the basic work from my designs and then I'd be adding the details and the paint etc etc. So, yes, I have to live there too and be on the site. But I'm only responsible for the details, not the main carving which would take me away for far too long.'

'But why can't you take Chiara with you?'

'And why can't Pina come too to look after us?'

The quiet audience had started to perk up.

Pina of course already knew the answer to Chiara's question but waited for Remo's reply with interest.

'School, cara. I can't uproot you from here, which is your home, at this time of your life. Come September, you'll be going into Miss Roche's class and then the 11+. I can't disrupt that.'

Chiara replied instantly: 'Oh no, I don't want to miss being in Miss.Roche's class. She's wonderful. We only have her now and then for French and music but we all love her and the top class says she's the best.'

'Exactly,' said Remo. 'You have to stay. But I don't have to go. This is what I meant when I sat you in that chair for supper: the decision, Chiara, is yours. This is where you learn to be mistress of this house.'

'But you have to go, Pappa. It will be good for you and your work. You hardly ever get to carve nowadays. And I'll be fine here with Pina and we'll see you in the holidays.'

The simple ways of a child! No major change to her pattern of life except that her father would be away. Her only parent would be away and yet she made so little fuss. And it was not that she didn't adore him. She did.

'Well, it seems, you've made your decision, cara,' said Remo, 'and now it's up to Pina to think about the changes it will make to her life and if she wants them.'

Pina nodded. 'I need to think about this very carefully. Don't worry, Chiara, whatever happens will be for the best.'

She spoke with confidence and a warm smile but her head was in a spin and her heart was pounding wildly.

'And now,' she said, 'no arguments. We'll all do the washing up!'

- Four-

'Bless me, Father…well…I haven't exactly sinned…but I need to talk to you privately.'

It was Saturday morning and Pina had waited until the last of those wanting to go to confession had left the church before she entered the confessional box herself.

'You know who I am, Father?'

'Of course, Pina, but why not come to the house if you just want to chat?' Fr Martyn asked.

'Because I want to talk to you privately and I don't want to upset Brigid by asking her not to be present. I don't mind her knowing eventually but not until I've sorted things out in my own mind.'

'Go ahead, Pina. I'm listening and this conversation has the privacy and sanctity of a confession.'

And Pina recounted the events of the previous Friday evening.

'So at no time has Remo mentioned his wife to you?' Fr Martyn asked.

'Never,' replied Pina.

'And your anxiety?' asked the priest.

'Is all about this change of situation,' she replied. 'What happens when he comes back? Do I move back to my sister's? What effect will that have on Chiara? He doesn't seem to have thought things through properly at all. If I refuse the offer, he'll turn down the commission. We both know he cannot and will not take Chiara to Italy with him for the reasons he's given and no doubt because he can't risk her finding out about her mother.'

'Who is your patron saint...*Giuseppina*?' asked the priest.

'Why, St Joseph, of course,' she replied, rather taken aback by his question.

'And what was his role in life?'

'Looking after...'

'Someone else's child. Yes, I see where you're going, Father.'

'And as to the future, let it take care of itself, my dear. Do what the present demands and let God take care of tomorrow.'

'I've not been entirely open with you,' Pina continued, 'and this part may count more as confession than conversation...'

'You don't have to say a word,' said the priest. 'You've developed feelings for both daughter and father, as was more than likely and very normal. They are fine feelings. Nothing to be ashamed of at all. How they will blossom, we don't know, but I'm the one who put you in that situation and I have no reason at all to be sorry that I did. So now, no penance, but just a blessing. May Almighty God, the father...'

- Five -

When Pina arrived on Sunday afternoon to make the supper, she found the table already set. No word was spoken and it was clear that Chiara had been instructed by her father not to mention anything about Friday's conversation. They went about their customary Sunday afternoon business. Remo read the papers, Chiara prepared her clothes for school on Monday and did a little more of her homework while Pina saw to the meal.

When they sat around the table again, with Chiara still occupying her father's chair, Pina spoke.

'No point in waiting until tomorrow to tell you. I've decided. Tell me when would be the best time for me to move my things from my sister's?'

Remo and Chiara had been holding their hands under the table out of sight. They shot their free hands now across the table to grasp Pina's which simultaneously went out open to them both. The family circle was complete.

Chiara

_____

'Pina?'

'Yes, Chiara.'

'Do you know Gabrielle at my school?'

'Yes of course.'

'Well, do you think I could have my hair in ringlets like hers?'

'Hmm. I don't want to say *no* but I think that's something for you to discuss with your father when he comes home. And can I just say, you'd have to get up even earlier in the morning to get them right...and so would I!'

'What do you mean?'

'Well they don't just happen. You have to use heated tongs and to be honest I don't think all that heat on hair is very good for it but if you really fancy ringlets...'

'Yes, well maybe I'll think about it a bit more...Pina?'

'Yes, Chiara.'

'Do you think we could go to Italy this summer?'

'Well, that depends a lot on your father's work.'

'No. I meant could we go and stay in your house with Lola and the girls. They told me last week they were thinking of going and I wondered...'

'There'd be room for us all, certainly, and it would be good, but with your father away so much in Italy these days, he might want to spend the summer here with you. So let's wait and see.'

'Will you ask him when you write next?'

'Yes of course, Chiara.'

This was a typical pattern for conversation between Chiara and Pina. Always reasoned and reasonable, nothing dismissed as out of hand without thought, even when rather odd or even outrageous.

- Two -

It was the start of the summer term and Chiara was coming to the end of her first year in the top class at the Convent. The influence of Miss Roche as her teacher had been very beneficial as predicted and hoped. Remo had returned regularly for a week or so at a time whenever Chiara was on holiday from school, but the commission occupied him fully in Italy and on his return he had little time other than for his making of a quantity of statuettes for his usual suppliers. He had to leave the painting of them to Chiara and even Pina turned her hand to basic colour painting but the fine features of faces and hands she left to Chiara who was often assisted at the weekends by Pina's two nieces – Franca and Rosa – and her sister Lola. There was quite a company in all gathered on a Saturday night and they always ate their supper together with Pina and Lola taking it in turns to prepare and cook. During this period, Chiara really got to know Lola's girls and the three became firm friends, almost inseparable when they were not at school.

- Three -

'Children, children, settle down now!' said the neat figure in the traditional navy blue dress with the little lace collar and the half moon silver brooch with its inset sparkling stones that the children always thought must be diamonds. The wispy grey hair sometimes escaped from the bun on her head but Miss Roche always seemed aware when even a little was out of place and a deft hand soon tucked it back.

'We have a letter to write this morning,' Miss Roche began, 'about what will be happening this term. We shall all try to write in the best handwriting we can as the letter is going to be taken home to your parents and we want them to be proud of how you write. I shall write it out on the blackboard and you must copy it neatly, taking care to keep within the lines printed on your papers. Now, give out the paper, please, Paul, and make sure the inkwells are full…yes…ah…yes, you can fill the wells, Maria. Be careful now, not too full. And no talking behind my back when I turn to the easel.'

My dear parents,
As we begin our new term…'

The chalk began its smooth neat white progress between the lines printed on the blackboard for writing practice. The reverse of the board was blank for sums and other exercises and was usually changed round at morning break but this letter copying would take quite a while.

'Excuse me, Miss Roche.'

The teacher paused and turned, relieved to have a moment's pause from writing in her best rounded writing which was always a strain.

'Yes, Chiara. How can I help?'

'Well, I'm not sure how to start the letter. I don't have parents, only a father and it never seems right to say *My dear father* as I always call him Pappa.'

'Well you can write that...with two 'p's.'

'Only two?'

'Oh very good...well, use three altogether, Chiara.'

'But, Miss Roche...'

The teacher was just turning back to the board.

'Yes, Chiara.'

'My pappa is in Italy and I should be giving the letter to Pina who looks after me.'

'Then write *My dear Giuseppina*,' said Miss Roche.

'Thank you, Miss Roche,' said Chiara, dipping her nib into the ink well with renewed vigour and concentrating hard on making her letters fit inside the guidelines on the paper.

At last the hand bell was heard being rung from the entrance hall where it sat next to the statue of St Anthony of Padua and not far from the white cane which all the children knew but few feared as it hardly ever stirred from its place.

'Quietly now,' said Miss Roche. 'Down to the Salle for your milk. I'll be down in a moment with Ovaltine tablets for those who would like them.'

When Pina went to collect Chiara that afternoon, she was presented with the letter neatly folded. It contained no more than dates of importance and a gently worded reminder that there would be school reports and accounts sent out in the latter part of the term.

- Four -

It was clearly a day for letters as when they opened the front door there was a letter from Italy lying on the mat. Initially the stamps had caught Chiara's eye and she thought there was a message for her from her father, but the printed sender's address on the envelope almost instantly wiped the interest from Chiara's face and she handed it to Pina without comment.

Pina's reaction however was less dismissive as she saw the words of the address. *Rifugio in dolore*: Refuge in Grief. And she realised that in one corner of the envelope, underlined boldly, were the words *PRIVATE* and *URGENT*.

With most correspondence that arrived during Remo's absence, Pina just opened and dealt with the contents but something stopped her from opening this one. Of course she knew where it was from but she could only speculate on its contents. Had Remo somehow forgotten to pay the fees? Was the refuge making an appeal? Had something significant happened? Of course curiosity prompted her to open it and then bluff her way through the consequences of such a decision. Reluctance to deal with the letter tempted her to tear it up and pretend it didn't exist, that it had never arrived. Trust in the providence that had put her into such a position brushed aside both courses of action.

'Chiara! I'll be gone for a little while,' Pina called out. 'Just slipping out to Exmouth Street.' And with that, taking her purse, Pina hurried out to the main Post Office at Mt Pleasant before it closed. She sent a telegram to Remo in Italy.

'Letter from Rifugio marked urgent. Please advise action.'

It was the following morning that the reply came, fortunately, after Pina had taken Chiara to school so there was no need for explanation or discussion. The message read:

'Destroy completely unopened. Home in 7 days.'

Pina took out the letter and turned it over again in her hands. There could be no doubt where it was from. Temptation such as afflicted Pandora edged her towards opening it. Indeed, she took out a knife from the kitchen drawer and slit the envelope so that she might cut out the stamps but even as she did so, she knew in her mind that she would not look at the contents. So when, without warning a small oblong card slipped out from the envelope onto the floor, she was taken by surprise. She picked it up to replace it inside the envelope and as she did so she could hardly fail to notice the black edging on the card surrounding a small old photograph of a young woman. Pina caught her breath, startled at what she saw.

It was the very image of how Chiara might look in ten years or so… and the young girl's hair was arranged in ringlets. She looked no further, replaced the card and neatly clipped the stamps from the envelope before thrusting it deep into the pocket of her *scousale*. She paused. The clock said nearly ten o'clock. She took out the letter again, quickly pulled on a coat, put the envelope in the pocket and dashed to church where she was just in time for morning Mass.

It must be said that her mind was less on the service than on what she needed to do and when Fr Martyn left the altar she waited for him to emerge from the sacristy. He smiled when he saw her and instantly asked, 'Confession, non-confession or coffee?'

'Coffee, please Father. And with Brigid too, if she's free.'

When the three of them were once again seated in the lounge, Pina began.

'It was here that you both took me into your confidence. Now it's my turn to do the same. This letter has come from Italy. Remo instructs me to destroy it unopened.' And she went on to describe what had just occurred. 'I want you both to know its contents in case he never tells you himself but then please destroy it for me. I'm sure that though it's in Italian you'll get the general meaning as I did when the card fell out.'

'Well, Pina,' said Brigid. 'I'm quite overwhelmed that you trust me with such information. It says a lot. Thank you. But now, how do you feel?'

'Very strange,' Pina replied. 'Here we are avoiding talking about something which has never been mentioned in all the years I've been in their house. And yet, now the situation has changed and I'm not sure what I'm supposed to do.'

'Do nothing,' said Fr Martyn. 'Just wait and react slowly to whatever happens when Remo returns. Remember Chiara is your priority and has been since you first arrived.'

- Five -

As the telegram had promised, Remo returned within the seven days. Pina had kept the fact that he would be returning a secret from Chiara and as he arrived on a school day, she packed him off to meet Chiara from school as an unexpected treat. He complied easily and it was clear from the excitement at the supper table that Chiara was delighted to have her father back home again.

'Now,' he began, once the dishes were cleared. 'What's this I hear about you wanting to come to Italy in the summer?'

Chiara shifted in her chair and glancing at Pina blushed a little.

'Well, Pappa, the girls are going to stay in Pina's house this summer and they asked me if I'd like to go with them. Pina and Lola said I had to ask you.'

'So you don't want to come where I live?' said Remo, pretending to look hurt, though in fact he was concealing his surprise. 'Hmm, very nice. Don't want to see what I've been working at so hard to keep you in luxury. Just want to have fun with your friends. What a lovely welcome!'

For just a second, Chiara didn't know what to make of her father's response, then she saw his face crack into a smile at the edges of his mouth and his eyes twinkle and she knew the truth, jumped up and hugged him.

'Of course, I want to see the statues. We can all be together for some of the time, can't we?'

'You can travel out with Lola and the girls and I'll bring you home with me when I come back in September. So Pina, will you go out with them all too? Is there room for you all in your house there?'

'Oh yes,' Pina replied. 'But I'm going to be selfish and let Lola go first and air the place…I'll spend a couple of weeks here doing jobs that I can't do while you're all around and then I'll come over to join you.'

Chiara went to bed very happy that night and when Remo and Pina were alone together, he pulled up his chair.

'Thank you so much, Pina, for all you've done while I'm away. I couldn't have taken this job without your help.'

Pina smiled and shrugged her shoulders a little in acceptance of what he had said.

'Can I ask?' he started again, hesitantly. 'About the letter? Did you…?'

'I disposed of it as you asked,' Pina replied looking straight into his eyes.

'Unopened?' he continued.

'Well…' she replied, glancing away, 'not exactly…' and she looked up and saw a flicker of concern cross his brow and his gaze becoming more intent.

'I did slit open the envelope,' she admitted and his eyes grew wider. But instantly she knew she was tantalising him a little cruelly and added, 'so that I could cut off the stamps for Chiara…and I disposed of the rest.'

And she saw the stiffness melt from his hunched shoulders as he glanced away to hide his embarrassment.

'Thank you, Pina. Thank you.'

- Six -

It was after supper the next evening that Remo produced three sheets of paper and looked severely serious.

'I was wondering if you could shed some light on this strange comment,' he began. 'I've been going through the paperwork that I've neglected while I've been away. Three of my regular customers for the statuettes have re-ordered but with a note, more or less the same from all of them: *'Could you include a few more teardrop Madonnas in the next batch as they are proving very popular?'* What on earth are *teardrop* Madonnas?'

He glanced from Pina to Chiara and back again and saw his daughter redden a little.

'I think Chiara should explain,' said Pina. 'After all, it was her idea.'

'I'm waiting,' said Remo with no lessening of the severity in his look.

'Well,' Chiara began. 'You know that the girls often come over on a Saturday and help me paint the statues? Lola and Pina help too. Lola does the lips perfectly and…well…anyway, I always do the eyes and one day I made a mistake with the thickness of the paint and when we checked later, it looked as if I'd painted a teardrop in the Madonna's eye. I was going to wipe it clean and paint over it and start again, but the others said to leave it and when it dried, it looked really good, so we…I, did a few more every now and then and included them with the ordinary ones.'

'I agreed they looked special,' said Pina.

'Fantastic!' exclaimed Remo, breaking into a smile and patting Chiara's head. 'Let's continue…so long as only you do the tear drop, Chiara. And every one like that that we sell will go into your savings fund as a little extra…but let's keep the number regulated, so they stay special, and put a mark on the base in future so we'll always know how many there are.'

– Seven –

The plans for the summer progressed easily as the term drew to its close. When she returned to school in the autumn, it would be Chiara's last year at the Convent. The 11+ loomed and the decision about which school she would attend next. Remo returned from Italy just once more and during this time, they discussed the final arrangements.

'Remo,' Pina began, one evening after Chiara had gone to bed, 'I have something on my mind that needs to be discussed. Your commission will be finished by the end of the summer? Am I right?'

'Why, yes,' he replied, quizzically.

'So you'll be here full time after that?'

'Of course.'

'Good. Well I think it might be best then if we reverted to our original pattern of living. I'll go back to Lola's and just come during the day as before.'

Remo looked stunned.

'I don't understand,' he said. 'Why change? This pattern suits us well.'

'I don't think I can really explain,' said Pina. 'It just feels that I should start getting back to normal.'

'Well, let's see how we go,' said Remo. 'Don't say anything to Chiara yet please, and let's have a summer without change hanging in the air over us. Would that be alright with you?'

'Totally fine,' Pina replied. 'I just wanted to let you know how I was thinking.'

- Eight -

When the *corriere* stopped at the bottom of the road that led up to the village, Pina was the only passenger to alight. She was a little surprised that there was no one waiting for her but the day was hot and there was no shelter along the main road and no guarantee that the corriere would arrive at a precise time so she thought to herself that her sister had been prudent in not letting the girls come to meet her.

One thing did take her breath away. An enterprising farmer had replaced the conventional maize crop with a field of sunflowers. They were tall now, thick stemmed and in full bloom already with a host of bees darting in and out of the sunny faces. They were so tall that they obscured the road uphill from view. Pina travelled lightly and so her cases were not a particular problem and she was cheered as she set off uphill towards her old home. The spire of the church was visible in the distance and she thought of all that had happened since she was last here.

Lost in her thoughts, she was startled as she rounded a bend in the road to come suddenly upon a familiar figure sitting by the roadside. A soon as she saw Pina, Chiara leapt to her feet and ran to her with arms open, flung them round her waist and hugged her.

Overwhelmed, and full of happiness at this reception, as she was, it took Pina a short while to realise that Chiara was sobbing into her embrace and when they disengaged, she saw tears streaming down the child's face.

'Whatever's the matter, cara?' she asked. 'What's happened?'

'Why didn't you tell me?' replied Chiara, sobbing. 'What have I done wrong? Why do you want to leave us? I don't understand.'

'What's all this?' said Pina. 'What do you mean?' she added calmly. Surely Remo hadn't said anything to his daughter after his request to

Pina to remain silent about her plans? It was he who had asked for silence on the matter. She couldn't believe that he had broken the silence himself.

'We were talking,' Chiara began between sobs, 'and Rosa and Franca both said you were going to be spending more time with them again when we went back. They were so pleased. And I asked Lola what they meant and she said she was getting your old rooms ready and…'

'And…and…and…' Pina interrupted. 'Nothing has been decided. It's just a thought. Don't let it spoil the holiday.'

'But why?' asked Chiara again. 'Why would you even think of such a thing? Tell me Pina.'

'I don't know, cara. Sometimes things last for a day, sometimes for a season and sometimes for a lifetime…and sometimes we just don't know which. Let me say this. Your father knows I've been wondering if he actually needs me to be around quite so much, now that he'll be back permanently after the commission. You managed very well, the two of you, and maybe he would like to have you all to himself again. Of course I'd still do things as we did before so it would make little difference to your daily life. Nothing much would change. It's not as if I'm intending to emigrate or come back to Italy. So dry your tears now, enjoy the sunflowers and let things take their own natural course. You know, Natty's been growing sunflowers in the garden in Granville Street and I think some of them are quite as tall as these here…maybe not so well advanced yet…'

'*Heavens above,*' thought Pina to herself. '*I'm sounding like a priest. Maybe I missed my vocation!*'

'So let me have one of the cases to carry,' said Chiara, 'and let's see what happens.'

Her tears dried on her cheeks but her pale smile did not reflect the sunshine of the flowers all around her.

- Nine -

The three weeks of holiday in the village stretched out ahead of Pina like a landscape with no horizon and she was very happy to be back at her family hearth and to have her sister with her and the younger generation as well but they could amuse themselves, and after a couple of days, Pina did the rounds of the village and talked to the ladies who now were responsible for the church cleaning rota.

She offered to resume her duties while she was living at home and they gladly accepted the break as a sort of holiday time for themselves.

On the third day after her return, Pina armed herself with her usual box of cleaning materials and a full new tub of beeswax polish and set off for the church. As she passed the priest's house, Padre Girolamo waved at her and beamed. He had already seen her at Mass and they had caught up with events when he had gone to supper with the family earlier in the week. He smiled to himself and wondered if Pina would be voicing her thoughts in front of the Madonna...but he was too discreet to make any attempt to find this out.

Pina slotted perfectly into her old routine, looking forward to concluding with the statue of the Madonna and child which now of course had more significance and interest for her than before in the olden days.

She finished polishing the pews and pulled out the priedieu, plumped up the blue kneeling pad and got ready to start her prayers. Perhaps a short litany, she thought, would give her aspects of the Madonna's life to contemplate rather than the repetition of a rosary. What she wanted to avoid was a discussion of her own situation. Somehow this was no longer an easy thing to start, much as she wanted to do so.

She had hardly begun when she glanced up at the face of the statue. What was that? Some specks of dirt on the Madonna's face. She would have to stop. She pulled out the steps to reach up to clean. To her amazement there was a speck of something in the statue's eye and a tiny trail down the cheek. It looked like a flow of tears. When she tried to clean them off, she realised that from the wood beneath the paint had seeped out some tiny drops of sap, of resin, and these had hardened but were easily chipped off with the edge of her nail and left no mark on the paintwork itself. There was no doubt however that the exit point for the resin had been the corner of the Madonna's eye. She said nothing about this phenomenon but every time she returned to clean during those weeks, there was a fresh drop in the eye, even though now that she was cleaning, it did not have the chance to trickle.

In the last week of the holiday, Remo arrived. He had hired a car and took the whole family out day after day on excursions, either to local towns when there was a market to enjoy or to the *Diga* for the girls to play in the water and on a couple of occasions as far as the coast at Cinque Terre which the girls especially loved. He lodged at the priest's house during his stay as there was no room for him at Pina's. But he knew Padre Girolamo from years back when he had worked on the statue in the church. He shared all his meals with the family. He was going to take Lola and the three girls to the airport before going back to finish his business for the commission and then return to London in time for Chiara's return to school for the new term. During her holiday she and Pina had been to visit Remo's workshop and had seen the Stations of the Cross that had taken him so much time and effort. They were beautiful. There was no mistaking Chiara's face in that of the child with her mother, and no mistaking Pina's face and body in that of the mother talking to Jesus.

Pina would stay on and put the house to bed, after Lola had left. There were no tears at the airport as everyone knew they would soon all be together again.

On their return to the village, Pina asked Remo about the statue's leaking resin and he gave it a closer look.

'Hmm,' he commented, 'a little strange after all this time...but I think I can deal with that.'

And with paintbrush and skill, the face was freshened and restored.

After a quiet supper together, Remo said his goodbyes. Pina had expected some reference to the situation that they would face on their return to London but he had not raised the topic, in accordance with his promise before the holidays had started.

Pina had a couple of days to herself, putting the linen away fresh and clean in moth-proof *bavoule*, as they called the strong wooden chests in their dialect, tidying and polishing and setting all in order once more. Somehow from the way that Lola and the girls had enjoyed the holiday, she knew that this would once again be a family home even if only at holiday time. They were already wondering if they could all go for Christmas. She was pleased. The house had the air of being enjoyed and loved once again.

She continued her church duties and just as Remo had predicted, the Madonna was no longer crying! On the day when she was due to catch the *corriere*, she had plenty of time to spare and so popped into church for a farewell chat. There was no one about as she pulled out her kneeler and settled at the feet of the statue.

She made the sign of the cross and glanced up at the statue's face, partly to check that the tears had really dried, and was so startled to see once again, tucked between the outstretched hands of the infant, a long envelope, curved to stay in place there.

There was no mistaking that her name *Giuseppina Busetta* was written across the front of the envelope.

Trembling, she stood up and took it from the infant's hands.

Trembling, she opened the slightly sticky back flap of the envelope and took out a single sheet of paper.

Trembling, she read the following words:

'Home is where your heart is cherished.
Home is where a daughter loves you.
Home is where you can be both mother and wife.
Giuseppina, come Home.'

- Ten -

It was with some trepidation that Pina alighted from the 38 bus in Rosebery Avenue and made her way past the Town Hall to the street she had come to regard as home.

She turned the key in the lock and the door creaked open. The house was silent. She put down her case in the hall and made her way to the kitchen.

The table was set for a meal. In the centre of the table stood a vase with three tall, golden-faced sunflowers.

Chiara and Remo were sitting, one on each side of the table, looking mischievous.

As she entered, they stood up and, still without a word, indicated to her the seat at the head of the table where her napkin had been laid.

She made her way to the chair, extended a hand to each of them, and pressed each hand in turn to her lips in a kiss and took her place. Chiara took her father's free hand in hers across the table and the three sunflowers illuminated the room with their joyous glow.

THE LITTLE WORLD
OF CHIARA ROMANI

Prologue

A New Day

'Pina?'

'Yes, Chiara, what's on your mind?'

'I was thinking about the wedding. Are you sure?'

'Sure about what, cara? Whether I want to get married?'

'No, I meant, sure about wanting it all to be so simple.'

'Yes, cara, both your father and I are happy with a simple ceremony. Aren't you? Are we being selfish and depriving you of a big occasion with a bridesmaid's frock?'

'No. I had enough with all that dressing up fuss for my first communion. I hated looking like a bridesmaid then and if I don't have to do that now, that would be fine. No, I just wondered if things were going to be special enough for you.'

'We've talked a lot about it, cara, and your father's concern is only, like yours, for the sort of day that will be special to me. That's why I have chosen a mid-week day so that we won't have to make a big deal of a party at a weekend.'

'But why are you having two ceremonies?'

'Well we thought it would be easier to do the registration at the Town Hall first and then go over to Church for a blessing. If we had it over a weekend we might have had to have a full nuptial Mass and a church full of strangers. This way we can keep things simple and low key and we can invite Fr Martyn...'

'And Brigid?'

'Of course and Brigid to lunch afterwards. You and Lola's girls are having the day off school as you know. We've cleared that with your teachers. Did I tell you...? Sister Angela's face when I told her I was going to be Mrs Romani was a picture! First she pursed up her lips and narrowed her eyes and stared hard at me through those little glasses...I saw her hands had frozen on the desk...but then she relaxed – first her hands and then her face – and she managed a smile of sorts as she looked away from me out of a window, waved her hand and said "Yes, yes of course Chiara can have the day off. Special permission granted… and the wedding will be in…Oh yes, Our Lady of Amwell of course, not St John's. So the dear Canon will not be marrying you." I said I hoped not as I'm marrying Mr Romani and wouldn't want to be a bigamist!'

Chiara laughed.

'Sister looked horrified. I don't think she appreciated my joke. She said she meant the Canon wouldn't be officiating at the wedding. "That will be your parish priest," she said. "Indeed it will, Sister," I said. I told her Fr Martyn and I were good friends and that it was he who introduced me to the family. Sister just smiled then and the conversation ended. So that's all settled then and Lola had no trouble with the girls being allowed to have time out either.'

'So the plan is to have lunch out somewhere? Do you know yet where?'

'Yes, cara. It's a wedding present…well a contribution to it. Natty's arranged for us all to have lunch at Casa Prada and our three lunches, yours, mine and your father's are her gift. You know she works in that restaurant as a waitress? Well her boss has given her time off and a special rate for those we invite so she'll be joining us as well and she'll enjoy being waited on for a change, maybe even by one of her cousins who are waitresses there. She'll relish that! Not having to do the job herself. She's been really helpful as well.

'You know her brother is married to a lady's tailor and dressmaker? Well, she's agreed to make me a new outfit for the wedding. Your father brought me some silk back from Florence a few visits ago, you know, that lovely material with the blue and grey pattern in it. He thought it might be enough for a skirt but when I took it to Natty's sister-in-law she said she could make me a full dress from it, with a little jacket as well. You have no idea how nimble fingered she is and how shrewdly she knows how to cut cloth. Hardly a scrap is wasted. All the smaller off-cuts are saved and she says they'll be used for piping and buttons. I've had a couple of fittings already and as long as I don't put on any weight, it will fit a treat! Her friend is a milliner and she's making me a small, a very small hat with a little bit of veil on it just to make the outfit complete.'

'That's the answer I was hoping for,' said Chiara, 'when I asked if you were sure. Now I'm sure you're really happy about things and I can look forward to the day as well. Can I just come in my school uniform?'

'Well, cara, I think our coupons will stretch to a new dress for you as well as a suit for your Pappa. After all I don't need mine at all. Let's go up West at the weekend and have a look for something for you which you'll enjoy wearing in the summer long after the wedding is forgotten!'

'Oh the wedding won't ever be forgotten,' said Chiara seriously. 'It's the best thing that's happened in this house since you first knocked on the door!'

A Record

'Pina?'

'Yes, cara.'

'Can you explain why we're having a festival? Is it like Christmas or Easter?'

'What are you talking about, cara? Something at school?'

'Well, we've been talking about it at school because there's going to be a photograph.'

'That's new,' replied Pina. 'We haven't had a letter.'

'That's because we haven't written it yet! But we were practising our best writing for it today.'

'So what did it say?' asked Pina.

'Well, to celebrate the festival in Britain the school's going to take a picture of us all this summer. Then it says about uniform and cost and dates but I don't remember all the details.'

'I'll see it when you've written it properly tomorrow,' said Pina. 'And now I know what you're talking about: it's the Festival *of* Britain not *in* Britain. The photograph will make a nice record.'

'How can a photo be a record?' asked Chiara.

'It's like the Italian word *ricordo*,' replied Pina. 'It means something to remember things by. You often see it on postcards in Italy. A sort of little reminder of something or somewhere.'

'So, it's not an actual record that you can play?' said Chiara.

'I don't think they've managed anything quite like that,' said Pina. 'A record with photographs on it. Now that would be fantastic. And impossible.'

'But what's it for?' asked Chiara. 'This festival, I mean?'

'To cheer us all up after the war,' replied Pina, 'and to encourage us to look forwards not backwards. I've read a lot about it in the papers. There's a new site being developed by the River called Festival Gardens.'

'But why now?' asked Chiara. 'The war's been over for years.'

'It's 100 years since there was a great Exhibition under Queen Victoria,' explained Pina.

'What was so special about that…' asked Chiara, 'that we want to celebrate it 100 years later?'

'It was a sort of show-case,' said Pina. 'To show the world what a great place Britain is.'

'Isn't that a bit show-offy?' said Chiara. 'And you always tell me it's not good to show off.'

'Sometimes countries have to show other countries that they're important and should be valued. I suppose we need to do that now after the war caused so much upset between countries. Of course 100 years ago we had an empire.'

'Is that why Britain is called Great?' asked Chiara.

'I think so,' replied Pina. 'But whenever anything or anyone is called Great, there's usually trouble or sadness.'

'Is that the punishment for being a show-off?'

'Well, I wouldn't see it quite like that,' said Pina, 'but I don't want you to start calling yourself Chiara the Great. Just imagine what extra words your father would add to that to keep you humble!'

'Oh yes,' laughed Chiara. 'Don't worry, I won't give him the chance!'

- Two -

The letter from the Convent duly arrived with all the details about the photograph which would be subject to it being a bright and a dry day and Pina duly sent in her acceptance. Uniform must be worn and of course for the girls it would be summer dresses but with a blazer as well. No one could remember ever having a whole school photograph before. It was quite an exciting occasion to anticipate and everyone knew it would take ages to organise so there wouldn't be lessons for long on that day.

Chiara hoped that it would be on a sewing day as she didn't much care for those long sessions. Well, she didn't mind the stitching and sewing and the embroidery and getting everything neatly presented. That was a challenge that she actually enjoyed. She didn't like the endlessly repeated Rosaries while they worked. She often thought of the radio programme *Music while you Work* and wished that they could have music instead of prayers. They were told that it was good to offer prayers while doing manual work but it was clear that the main purpose was not to *hail Mary* but to keep the girls from hailing one another, chatting and becoming unruly. Of course the girls themselves were only partly aware of this.

When they grew up, the majority of them avoided occasions when the Rosary was recited with a determination that seemed disproportionate to the act of prayer itself. Chiara could never understand why Mary had to be hailed so repeatedly, and after trying to explain without a lot of success how the words acted as a sort of blotting out of the world around, Pina gave up and just reverted to the time honoured *You'll understand when you're older.* Anyway, the date for the photograph was too far off to know if it would blot out *Sewing*, but Chiara lived in hope.

- Three -

The excitement that the Festival generated caught everyone's imagination and Remo decided that the family should go. Pina was anxious about the expense involved. Entry to the great Dome of Discovery was as much as five shillings for a grown-up, but as Remo said, 'It's a once in a life-time. We'll go early and get our money's worth.'

'Can we go on the tram?' asked Chiara.

'We can walk,' said Pina. 'It's not that far to the River from here.'

'No,' said Remo, 'we'll go by tram. We'll need our energies for walking about especially if we go over to Battersea in the evening for the fireworks.'

'The tram is a treat as well,' said Chiara. 'It goes underground in Southampton Row and then it's like being on the underground except you're on a bus, a double-decker, until it comes out under the bridge.'

'We'll easily walk to the site from there,' said Remo. 'It'll be good to see all that bomb damage cleared up at last.'

'But it's only temporary,' said Pina. 'I don't think they'll keep the buildings.'

'I'm sure they will,' said Remo. 'After all, the cost is running into millions already.'

'Millions?' said Chiara.

'Yes, you have to spend to accumulate sometimes,' said Remo. 'It's all going to be in our best interests in the long run. You'll see.'

- Four -

The day of the excursion was slow in arriving. Something anticipated occupies the mind which starts a sort of countdown to the time of its actually happening. Chiara listened to whatever she could about the Festival on the radio and read about the features in the papers and was determined that whatever her father had meant by 'once in a lifetime' would be thoroughly investigated.

In the event, it was one single feature that stuck in her mind and that was a clock. There was so much to see and take in and the day was extended into the darkness as Remo had promised by crossing over to Battersea Park for the fireworks.

At school after the weekend of the visit, the children were asked, as usual, to write an essay about what they had done and Chiara knew that she would have to choose just one thing of all she had seen or else the essay would be too long. So she chose the clock.

'Excuse me, Miss Roche,' she began, raising her hand.

'Yes, Chiara. How can I help?'

'Would you put a spelling on the board for me, please?'

'Of course,' replied the teacher, reaching for her chalk. 'What is the word?'

'Guinness,' said Chiara.'I don't know how many 'n's and 's's there are.'

'My goodness!' said Miss Roche with the slightest suggestion of a twinkle. 'Fancy you wanting to write about that. Is it quite suitable, do you think?'

'Well it's what the clock is called,' said Chiara, 'and I must get it right.'

'Quite so,' said Miss Roche, writing the word on the board.

As the children worked on in silence, they hardly noticed the classroom door opening.

As usual, Sister Angela managed to move noiselessly through her domain and appear at unlikely moments in unlikely places.

Miss Roche looked up from her desk where she was quietly correcting the sums which the children had been doing earlier in the morning. When she noticed the head's figure in the doorway, she fingered her little moon brooch and made to rise, but Sister Angela motioned her to stay and then pointed to the word on the board. He face configured an expression of outrage as she turned and retreated from the door.

Miss Roche smiled and sighed; she knew that she would be quizzed later and toyed with the idea of saying that she was doing a project on public houses and the evils of drink, but she knew there would only be a major sense of humour failure and so it would be better to be prosaic in her response.

At least it was a diversion from the humdrum.

Meanwhile Chiara was hard at her task. Since seeing the clock, she had been fascinated by the way it worked and she had sorely tried Remo to offer her an explanation. He had done his best and had looked up as much as he could find about the mechanics involved.

The first viewing of the clock was the most exciting because it was not at all clear what was going to happen and the various elements took you by surprise. Chiara had been particularly charmed by the presence of the Mad Hatter from the Alice stories, though Remo couldn't understand why he was there at all as no other Wonderland figures appeared. Pina had preferred the Zoo Keeper but there had been a burst of applause from all the bystanders when the central doors opened and the toucans waltzed around.

The fish appearing one after the other along the fishing line, smaller and smaller as they emerged from the one below's open jaws in turn was funny too and seeing them have to go back at the end of the performance was just as funny. Remo said he was disappointed that there was no animation for the glass that gets stuck in the neck of the ostrich in the common advertisements for the drink. And then he wished he had remained quiet as Chiara leapt on that and told him that it was within his powers to animate it and that would be a great idea…until he pointed out that once the glass had descended into the bird's stomach it would be ungainly for it to have to reappear by travelling up the bird's neck; it would seem that the ostrich was being sick. This soon lost its appeal and he could breathe again.

It was two days later, after Chiara had finished her essay that disaster struck. Little did she know that she would not be returning to school for over two weeks.

- Five -

'Pina, could you look at my chest?' Chiara asked at bath time. 'It's been very itchy today.'

Pina looked at the light rash. 'It may be nothing…just a heat rash,' she said. 'See how it feels in the morning.'

But by the morning there was no doubt. The rash had spread to Chiara's face.

Remo took one look at breakfast. 'No school for you, cara. That's varicella.'

'Chicken pox,' added Pina. 'There will be no school for quite a while. You're contagious.'

'What does that mean?' asked Chiara, looking a little scared.

'Chicken pox is very catching,' explained Pina. 'It means that if you go into school, other children may develop the rash as well. You probably picked it up from someone there who didn't know they had it. You don't want to be passing it on to your friends. These spots will soon turn to blisters and when they break, there will be scabs. So we've got to see that you don't scratch yourself – particularly your face – or you might be scarred.'

'That's frightening,' said Chiara, immediately touching her cheek where there was an outcrop.

'How to stop you scratching?' Pina pondered. 'I suppose that until I can get to the chemist we could put something on to stop the itching. Maybe a dab of butter just for now.'

'What!' said Remo in mock horror. 'Surely you're not going to use my butter ration. I haven't had my toast yet this morning!'

'It might stop them drying out,' said Pina, 'and becoming too irritating.'

'I suppose I shall have to sacrifice myself again for the sake of my daughter!' Remo replied, hunching his shoulders in dejection and making Chiara laugh.

'Just until I get something from the chemist,' Pina added. 'But first, it's best if we cut your nails right back so there's nothing sharp there to break the skin.'

'Maybe Chiara could wear gloves,' suggested Remo, 'or mittens.'

'I have some thin cotton gloves,' said Pina. 'Better than mittens so Chiara can draw or write. Boredom is going to set in very quickly with being confined to the house.'

'You mean I can't go out?' said Chiara. 'Or see the girls?'

'Absolutely not,' replied Pina. 'I'll check at the chemist's and we may have to call in a doctor.'

'Do you have any books from the library?' asked Remo.

'No, Pappa. We took them back early last week and there was nothing on the shelves I fancied.'

'Just as well,' said Pina. 'They say that sometimes books can carry the germs and they need to be disinfected. One of us had better inform the school,' she said, turning to Remo. 'I'll pop in later and let them know. Meanwhile it might be best if we washed all her clothes and towels in case germs are lurking there.'

'I'll see to that while you're out,' said Remo. 'And what do you think you might do, Chiara, to pass the time while you're stuck at home? Any ideas?'

'I could do some painting for you on the statues, if that's alright.'

'Yes,' said Pina, 'but as soon as you start to feel tired, you must stop and you must wear the gloves. Let's see how you manage with a paintbrush when you have the gloves on. Let me go and find them now, while I remember.'

Pina left the kitchen and soon returned with a pair of thin white cotton gloves. 'Try these,' she said. 'They may be a bit big. I'll take the bus to Selby's at Nag's Head and see what they have in your size. These will do for now. Can you see to lunch, Remo? I may be gone a while.'

'Of course,' replied Remo. 'But we'll wait for you to come back before we eat.'

'And I've just thought,' said Chiara excitedly. 'I can listen to *Mrs Dale's Diary* and *Worker's Playtime* and…'

'There's not much wrong with you, cara,' said Remo. 'And you'll be on your own for the diary. I don't think I can cope with Mrs Freeman and her captain. I might manage *Worker's Playtime* depending on the comedian. If it's Arthur Askey, you'll be on your own again. Now, on with those gloves.'

'I'll be off then,' said Pina. 'Bye, cara. No kisses today!'

And off she sped leaving father and daughter to their own devices.

She liked the Chemist's in Amwell Street, run by Mr Davis who always had good advice. So she headed in that direction first, just briefly calling in to Our Lady of Amwell on the way to light a candle and say a prayer.

The chemist was his usual affable self and having heard Pina's description of the rash, agreed with her that it was likely to be chicken pox. He suggested calamine lotion and produced a large bottle of pink liquid.

'Don't use this on her face,' he warned, 'and keep it away from her eyes.'

'Is it safe to dab the spots on her face with butter?' asked Pina.

Mr Davis looked puzzled. 'If you find it soothes, I suppose so,' he replied. 'If you've butter to spare!' he added. 'You can dab the spots elsewhere with the lotion as often as you like. It's a good idea to bathe her every four hours or so, but take care when drying her. Only pat her dry. Don't rub or you'll spread the spots and the scabs may become nasty. Also, it might be wise to keep her out of the sun. Do you still have the black-out curtains up since the war?'

'Yes, Chiara's room gets a lot of sun so we left them up.'

'Good, use them to keep the room cool and shady,' said Mr Davis. 'And at night, put socks over her hands so that she can't scratch inadvertently. You should see things start to improve after about a week. You don't need to call in a doctor unless she develops other symptoms. But you'll find that her energy levels will sink and she'll want to be in bed more than usual. I've given you a large bottle of calamine but I think you'll need another before the rash has passed.'

Pina thanked the chemist and, looking round the comforting shop with its big coloured glass bottles and wooden shelves with their drawers, she smiled contentedly, feeling on top of what she had to do next.

- Six -

She crossed the street, passed through Myddleton Square and across Rosebery Avenue to the narrow lane in front of Dame Alice Owen's school. She walked by the gardens in Duncan Terrace and reached the school. Classes were in progress so there was a general hum of activity with occasional burst of laughter as she made her made up to Sister Angela's office. She tapped on the door and was invited in.

Sister did not rise to greet her visitor.

'Ah, Miss – I mean Mrs – Raimondi,' the nun started.

'Romani,' corrected Pina, 'Chiara's mother.'

'Of course, of course,' the sister flustered. 'How can I help?'

'Chiara is not in school today and may be away for the next two weeks,' explained Pina. 'We believe she has chicken pox.'

Sister Angela did not look at all perturbed. 'You are not the first to tell me this,' she said. 'Several mothers have called in with similar situations. You are wise to have kept her at home. Of course, I don't know where this strain of the trouble originated. It is passed on so very quickly among children. It could have come from anywhere. And so many families are visiting the festival these days. I am sure that it is likely to have originated there.'

'I'm not blaming the school,' Pina reassured her. 'I was just wondering if there are any text books I might borrow so that Chiara won't fall behind with her sums particularly as they are her weak spot. Her father and I could monitor her answers.'

'I don't think that is possible,' replied the nun. 'If I give out to one parent, others will want the same. Our stocks of books are limited and then there's the risk of infection through contagion. I know,' she put up her hand to stem argument, 'I know that there are people who say that this is not a reality, but I don't want to risk infection through contagion. I don't want to create an epidemic in Duncan Terrace, as I'm sure you'll appreciate,' she concluded with a rather forced smile.

'Yes indeed, Sister,' Pina replied as she prepared to leave.

'Let us hope that this will soon pass,' said the nun, shuffling her papers. 'And my best wishes to Chiara,' she added, half embarrassed that she was allowing herself to reveal a little warmth or sentiment.

When Pina finally arrived home from Nag's Head, it was clear that Chiara's condition had worsened. Remo had sent her to bed and had pulled down the old black-out curtains as the sun was quite fierce. Pina sat down and over a welcome cup of milky coffee she told Remo about her morning.

'Did you mention the school photograph?' he asked.

'No,' replied Pina, 'It slipped my mind completely. I am sure there'll be no trouble in cancelling the order for it when Chiara returns if she misses the day. It's a pity, I know, but what would she look like anyway covered in spots?'

– Seven –

The days passed slowly for Chiara: her treat was the constant stream of radio programmes that she usually only heard when she was on holiday from school. *Worker's Playtime* was a favourite and it proved to be a bright spot in her day. However, during this period of being confined to the house, she was destined to be disappointed. She always hoped to catch a broadcast when the bill was topped by Gert and Daisy. Something had taken her fancy about the way that Elsie and Doris Waters conducted their gentle exchanges about life and their husbands. They had been popular during the War years and had broadcast a lot then and their appearances were less frequent now so Chiara had missed their heyday and their broadcasts now were a rare treat. They usually concluded their act with a comic song, sometimes re-shaping the lyrics to their own tastes or situations. Chiara was often annoyed that she couldn't remember all the verses after only one hearing. The two weeks that she was at home did not produce a treat of this kind however. She had to content herself with other performers.

The radio was a boon but Pina was careful to ensure that there were breaks in the day when Chiara either read or rested or did a few basic sums. Writing wasn't so easy after all with the gloves on but they certainly solved the problem of scratching the itches on her face and the little dabs of butter certainly helped with the irritation. At night, she wore mittens, tied with ribbons at the wrists.

Pina always kept a supply of books in a cupboard. There were always too many at Christmas and Birthday times and so she secreted some away for times just like this when they could appear to while away the time with something new.

During the second week of confinement, Remo had the brilliant idea of popping up to the big record store HMV in Oxford Street and there he sought out an eclectic selection of 78s for Chiara's amusement. He went through the catalogue of what was available for children. He found a version of *the Wooden Horse of Troy* and some scenes from the *Alice* books with a child actor whose voice was familiar from Children's favourites singing *Christopher Robin* poems. The *Alice* records had other actors who often appeared on *Worker's Playtime*, including Arthur Askey. 'Oh well,' he thought, 'the sacrifices we make for our children!' Remo knew that Chiara would love identifying the voices. It would make for a good quiz game, he thought.

And then he thought of Chiara's disappointment at not hearing her favourite performers and he signed his own 'No more Peace' warrant as he asked the assistant if they stocked any recordings by Gert and Daisy and was duly handed, with a wry smile, a copy of *Everyone keeps pinching my butter.*

If only he had listened to it first, he might have thought it through properly but once it was secure in its brown paper sleeve and tucked away innocuously with the others, his fate was sealed.

Of course the records were a great hit with Chiara and, eked out over several days, they saw her through to the disappearance of her pox.

- Eight -

On her return to school, she learnt with disappointment that the photograph had been taken while she was confined at home.

Pina made an appointment to see Sister Angela on the following day.

As Pina tapped on the door, a curt 'Enter' emanated from the office. The nun was seated at her desk as usual facing the door.

'How may I help you?' she enquired without indicating to Pina that she might sit down, a sure sign that the interview should be short.

'I just wanted to assure you that Chiara is clear of the spots and fit to be back at school and to say that she is sorry to have missed the photograph...'

And before Pina could say more, the nun raised her hand imperiously.

'I'm afraid the answer has to be *no*,' she said.

'But you haven't heard the question, if there was one...' said Pina.

'Oh yes I have,' rejoined the nun. 'Several times from other parents, like yourself whose child missed the occasion. I cannot offer a refund for photographs ordered.'

'But I didn't want a refund,' said Pina. 'I wanted to say, if you had allowed me to finish, that I wanted to pay for my copy and collect it today if possible.'

The nun's expression was confounded and she turned pink in her confusion and sought to cover it by turning to a table near her desk where envelopes were stacked.

'Ah yes, here it is,' she said. 'Ready for you.'

Pina opened her purse to take out the right money, saying, 'I know that in years to come Chiara will appreciate having a record of all her fellow pupils even if they won't have a record of her.'

'Quite so, quite so,' replied the nun, taking the payment and having the grace not to check its accuracy before putting it into a cash box on her desk.

'Thank you, Mrs Romani,' she said without hesitation over the name. 'Your support is most welcome.'

'Good day, Sister,' said Pina, carefully putting the envelope into her shopping bag as she turned to the door, where she paused for a moment and looked steadfastly at the seated nun.

'Perhaps next time I call,' she said, 'you will have the grace to offer me a seat, seeing that our support is so welcome. It is always good to feel welcome when one goes calling.'

And with that she passed through the door and closed it firmly behind her without waiting for an answer.

- Nine -

During her confinement, Chiara had been excited by the continuing story line in *Mrs Dale's Diary* about the appearance of a ghost. Mrs Mountford, always a favourite caricature of a character had been much in evidence during this plot line and Monument, the gardener, had also been up to his tricks with a sheet, so it was all very light hearted and appealing. Once back at school, Chiara ruefully resigned herself to only hearing Pina's version of events but was at least consoled that Gert and Daisy had not decided to entertain factory workers the minute she had gone back to school. However it had been necessary to limit the number of times that she was allowed to play the record her father had bought, before either Pina or Remo or indeed both were carried off to Colney Hatch.

One evening before bed-time the family was all sitting round quietly when Chiara asked.

'Would you mind if I played Gert and Daisy, just once?'

Remo sighed and Pina stared hard at him with the look that said, 'Well, you brought this on yourself, didn't you!'

'You see,' Chiara continued, 'I've changed some of the words, with help from Pina, and another source, and I'd like to sing you my version,'

Pina looked away, not daring to catch Remo's eye.

How could he refuse? 'And what source might that be?' He asked.

'Well, Pina noticed on the record label that the words were written by Annette Mills... you know... the Annette Mills that talks to Muffin the Mule?'

Remo tried to show that he knew what Chiara was talking about but Muffin the Mule was not part of his wider general knowledge, so he just nodded.

'So I wrote a letter to Miss Mills and told her about having the spots.'

Remo waited.

'And I mentioned that I liked the Gert and Daisy song, as well as Muffin the Mule, and she wrote back, well her secretary did, with some suggestions for changing the words to fit the situation.'

'That was exceptionally kind,' said Remo, now impressed and more alert.

'So, can I sing them to you?' asked Chiara.

Remo opened his hands, resigned, and smiled.

So the gramophone was wound up and the needle checked and as it was set in the groove, the opening bars were played and Chiara began:

'Everyone is after my butter. They all want my butter for toast.
But there's nothing better than butter, wherever a spot itches most.
People love calamine lotion but I have this much better notion.
When my spots start to scab, to prevent me looking drab,
I don't leave my butter alone-one-one. I don't leave my butter alone.'

Home Movie

There was a reason why Pina did not like October. It had started as an unidentifiable feeling that she experienced every year since she had moved back to London. Was it because of the sad memory of her mother's death in an October years ago? Not really. That memory would bring a feeling of sadness at any time. Was it the autumn with its false cheerfulness of colour as the trees blazed out in rich russets and deep copper and caught the sun and took your breath away with its beauty until you realised that this was the dying year and that soon there would be bleakness for months until April opened up the freshness of a new one? No, for once someone had suggested that the old leaves were being pushed out by the new growth in the branches and that their falling was to make way for fresh growth, she had been able to adjust to the season's decay.

Decay!

That was the reason, or part of it: the smell of autumn, of must, and of mushrooms. The heavy overpowering smell of the porcini, the wild mushrooms gathered and laid out to dry indoors until the insect life in them had crawled out and their softness had turned to dry brown and yellow and white and they could be jarred and stored for the year ahead.

Mushrooms – *funghi* or *fauns*, as they were called in the dialect of the North – are the speciality and delicacy of so many families who had transferred their lives but not their tastes and habits from Italy to England. They delighted in the discovery that those very same mushrooms which they had believed were only in their northern hills had preceded their coming to foreign lands and were to be found in woods and near waters on the outskirts of the great metropolis.

They were not easy to find, but seeking them out and bringing them home in triumph was an autumn exercise that many families practised and the locations visited were kept as secret as possible from one family to another so that a reasonable crop might be harvested in due season. But if an expedition proved to be a failure, then the spoils were shared so that no one missed out on the bounty that added a dimension of excitement to the blandest of risotto meals.

But as she reflected on her dislike of autumn, Pina realised there was another reason for her discomfort as October loomed. There was always the chance of a letter arriving for Remo. A letter, a request, an invitation, an enquiry, a summons: it took different forms but whatever shape it assumed it meant the same thing: he would leave London for Italy for a couple of weeks or more. It was specialised work for which he was noted. In London his main source of income was from the ceramics he produced. But the better money – the money that lifted the household income into being able to afford luxuries and treats – came from his specialised work abroad, sometimes in Italy and sometimes in France. So whenever the letter arrived, there was never any discussion, no matter how much it disturbed Pina to be without Remo's company for these weeks. Chiara had adapted more easily and indeed she thought little of her father's autumnal disappearances especially since he had married Pina and her daily life was hardly disturbed at all. Such is the way it should be for a child growing up: security and such regularity that nothing disturbs their hearts and minds. And Remo had ensured that this was the way in which his daughter's life would develop in spite of his own disturbed pattern.

It was Friday and as they gathered round the supper table, Chiara noticed that the wellington boots were out of the cupboard and standing in a corner of the kitchen with a basket and some bags.

'So where are you off to tomorrow, Pappa?'

'Ah, you've noticed,' Remo replied.

'Of course,' said Chiara, 'and anyway Pina bought some of the cheese you like to go with the rolls she made today for your snack.'

'An early start?' asked Pina, already knowing the answer.

'Yes, the boys will pick me up about 5 tomorrow,' said Remo, 'and it's off to Virginia Water. But no word of this. We might get a second trip next weekend as well. It depends. The weather's been just right. So we don't want to let on where we're headed in case others get there before us!'

'When can I come too?' asked Chiara.

'No children,' said Remo. 'It's a rule. Adults only.' He smiled. 'There's a reason and it's a good one. Children rush about, not looking where they run and they do more damage to those places where the mushrooms hide. In a year or two, Chiara, I'll take you. It's important you learn how to spot good from poisoned mushrooms, But not this year. Anyway, your day is already planned as I understand.'

'Yes,' said Pina, 'we're going to see the new baby. Lola's coming too but we'll have supper on our own here this week when you come back.'

'Rather you than me,' said Remo. 'I've no wish to see a new baby, especially this one with all the fuss about it.'

'What fuss?' asked Pina. 'I know Natty had some trouble giving birth but…'

'Yes well,' said Remo. 'There's trouble and there's trouble. No doubt you'll hear the full story. I have several times already.'

'Ah, of course,' said Pina. 'You see Natty's husband at the Merlin's Cave when you pop in for a drink, don't you?'

'Yes and her cousins too sometimes. It was all a big drama apparently but I won't spoil it for you both.'

'It was you who told us there was going to be a baby back in February. I heard it from you before Natty told me herself.'

'Oh yes, and what a performance that was! There were a few of us in the Merlin's and Roberto came in with his overcoat draped over his shoulders as if it were a cape and he got out his wallet and opened it on the bar and said to the assembled company: "Drinks are on me tonight. Whatever you fancy. My wife is with child." He then waved his hand over the wallet which was full of notes and said to the barman "Take whatever you need." '

'I remember you telling us that, Pappa,' said Chiara, 'because at school the year before, Tonio was telling us about his Zia — that's Natty.'

'How did that go?' asked Pina. 'Remind me.'

'Well, Tonio said that he was round at his Zia's…he goes there a lot with his parents…and she asked him if she should have a baby or a television. Which would he prefer? He just shrugged his shoulders but a week or so later, she had a television. It was quite funny, but good for us because we get to go and see it when we visit!'

They all laughed.

'And now there's a baby,' said Chiara, 'I hope Zia Natty didn't give back the television!'

'Far from it,' said Pina, 'so you'll not have to sit and listen to all the grown ups' chit chat all the time.'

'Rather you than me,' said Remo. 'I'll take a day out in a damp wood looking for *fauns* any day.'

'Well if there were really fauns, you know, like baby deer or those little men with goats' legs, I'd rather come with you too,' said Chiara. 'But as they're only maybe poisonous mushrooms, I'm happy to leave them to you and go and see a baby.'

- Two -

The door in Granville Street was opened slowly and Roberto peered round it into the street to see who had knocked. When he recognised Pina, he put his finger to his lips and opened the door wider. 'Come in, come in. Lovely to see you, Pina, and you too, Chiara. Natalia's just resting but if you wait here, I'll see if she's awake.' And leaving them in the long narrow hallway, he walked solemnly to the door at the end by the stairs that led to the basement. He opened it very slowly and entered, closing it firmly behind him. Chiara and Pina looked at each other and shrugged their shoulders, with mystified expressions.

It was certainly a few minutes before Roberto returned and waved them forward into the bedroom.

It was a large room with double windows that looked out over the back gardens. In the fireplace the glow of the coals added light and warmth to the room and in the large double bed, facing the windows lay the diminutive form of Natalia. As Pina and Chiara entered, she seemed to be asleep or at least in repose, propped up against white pillows and positioned centrally in the bed. The white edge of the linen sheet was turned back over the counterpane, perfectly smooth, and on it lay her hands. Chiara noticed them before anything else as they were finely manicured and bright with what looked like a fresh coating of very bright nail varnish.

Pina's attention was attracted by the pink crocheted bed jacket with its edging of pink ribbon threaded through.

For a moment or two nothing happened and then, deferentially approaching the bed, Roberto whispered, 'Darling, you have visitors.' And the small head shifted as if from deep slumber and raised itself. The eyes opened and Natalia greeted her visitors with a radiantly sweet smile from her perfectly shaped and lipsticked rosebud lips.

'How lovely to see you, Pina, and you too Chiara. So kind of you to come. Pull up a chair. Roberto will be pleased he can go off duty for a while. He's being so wonderful. I don't know how I would have coped without him here during the day, and my sister-in-law comes in the evening.'

'I'll leave you to the ladies, darling,' said Roberto taking the chance of a hasty departure before it was withdrawn, and pulling two chairs to the side of the bed. 'If you need anything, just send Chiara down for me. If there's anyone at the door, perhaps she could answer it. I'm going to have a quiet read of my cowboy book and I may doze. I'll bring you up some tea later.' And he swiftly left the room.

'So,' began Natalia animatedly, without waiting to be questioned, 'you'll be wanting to know why I'm laid up like this. Total rest. That's what all the doctors ordered at the hospital after the operation. Total rest. No argument. So apart from feeding baby which I try to do my best to do well.' And she smoothed her hand over her breast as she spoke and lowered her eyes modestly. 'Apart from feeding my child, I do nothing else until I am told. Of course, it's hard on Roberto having to work nights until late. He doesn't get back until the early hours and then there's not much sleep for him until he has to start taking care of us again.' At the word *us* Natalia waved her hand generally in the direction of a corner of the room away from the fire where stood a substantial cot – or rather a cradle – on rockers, festooned with more of the pink ribbon that edged her bed jacket.

'*Well, the Amwell ladies have been doing good business with their ribbon,*' thought Pina who was already only half listening to Natalia's monologue, knowing full well that there was more to come and hoping that Lola would not be long in appearing, otherwise it was more than likely that she would have to hear this all over again. She re-tuned into Natalia's account somewhere in the middle of 'hospital bed being uncomfortable'. And she noticed that Chiara was giving wide-eyed attention to all the details and was getting especially attentive as Natalia approached the subject of the operation itself.

'I tried and tried,' Natalia continued. 'They told me to push but I just did not have the energy. It's taken all my strength to go full term and at the end there was nothing left. Nothing. I was in agony and in my pain I told them…you'll have to take the baby from me…I can do no more…'

And as she relived the moment, she flopped back onto her pillows and closed her eyes.

Chiara and Pina looked at each other and waited, the suggestion – just the suggestion – of a smile forming on each of their faces. They had no idea how long the eyes would remain shut and so instinctively they did not allow the smiles to develop.

Pina took the initiative and after a few seconds patted Natalia's hand. She rallied…and continued…

'I'm fine. I'm fine.' And from underneath her pillow she took a delicate little handkerchief to dab her eyes which were moist. Pina could not help noticing that the handkerchief was edged with pink ribbon, of a narrower gauge than had been used on the bed jacket but of exactly the same shade.

'And so well looked after by my Roberto. What a trial I must be to him, but now you must see that it has all been worthwhile. Please, go and see the baby.' And she directed their gaze with a gentle wave of her hand towards the cradle. On rockers. With a canopy built over the top in a triangular shape, draped with lacy, filmy linen and decorated with festoons of pink ribbons that seemed to invade the whole room.

Chiara was first out of her chair to see the occupant of this fairy tale crib and had trouble actually finding it under the swathes of linen. But just visible was the small pink face and one tiny hand, belonging to a child in angelic repose. Pina joined Chiara and both admired the new arrival with suitable comments and noises. When they glanced back at Natalia, they saw that her eyes had closed again.

Then suddenly, there was the sound of the knocker on the front door. Sharp raps, and instantly Natalia was upright and perky.

'That might just be Lola,' said Pina. 'She said that she might meet us here today if she could. Go and answer the door, cara, and save Roberto coming upstairs again.'

'Yes, yes,' said Natalia, 'please answer it and just wait a few moments before bringing her in.'

Chiara made towards the bedroom door as Natalia said to Pina, 'Please, bring me the baby now. She needs her mother.'

And puzzled but compliant, Pina lifted the sleeping baby out of the cradle and brought her over to Natalia who was suddenly a picture of liveliness as she plumped up and smoothed her pillows, unaided, and opened her arms to receive her child, carefully arranging the long baby robes artistically across the counterpane so that by the time that Chiara had opened the bedroom door to admit Lola, Natalia was a perfect magazine picture of motherhood.

Lola and Pina greeted each other with a kiss and Pina whispered, tapping her watch. 'I'm off...meet you at Lyons...about an hour... you'll see why.' And then, out loud to Chiara, 'Just pop down and tell Roberto not to trouble with tea for us. You remember...' and she opened her eyes wide as she spoke looking directly at Chiara, 'you remember what I said I would get done before your father gets back. It slipped my mind until now.'

As Pina kept her eyes very wide and very open, Chiara caught her meaning and swiftly started to put on her coat. And not a moment too soon as the infant, disturbed from its rest, realised that it was no longer comfortable and began a wail.

'Sorry to rush off, Natty,' said Pina, 'but we only wanted to pop in and see you and we mustn't tire you and you have Lola for company now.' And she looked at her sister whose face was turned away from the bed towards Pina as she mouthed silently the words *'Thanks a lot!'* and then returned with a sweet smile to the adoration of mother and child.

Chiara was soon back from seeing Roberto downstairs and Pina's coat was buttoned up. She blew a kiss to mother and child.

'Oh,' said Chiara, 'but we don't know what name you've given her.'

Natalia replied as she attempted without success to rock the infant back to slumber and silence, 'She's my little angel, sent from heaven, so we are calling her Angelina.'

And waving her goodbyes, Chiara followed Pina out of the room, in silence to the front door. Once it had closed with a bang behind them, they both looked at each other and gave a great burst of laughter which they had been suppressing.

'And these jobs, you have to do for Pappa, Pina?' asked Chiara.

'Erm, well,' replied Pina, 'I might just remember them if I have a nice cup of tea somewhere first. Come on, Chiara! Let's go to the Angel and see what Lyons has on offer this afternoon. If nothing else, I think we deserve a bag of peppermint creams.'

- Three -

It might not have been as much as three quarters of an hour before Lola joined her sister and Chiara at the Lyons cafe and Restaurant, at the Angel. Everyone called it the Corner House, because it was on the corner, but in fact if you referred to it as such, the staff were quite snooty about it and corrected you as it was unique in the chain of Lyons properties, not as lowly as a tea shop but not as grand as a Corner House, and so rather special in its own right, and much loved by the inhabitants of Islington.

'I had to leave,' Lola exclaimed. 'I couldn't stand the noise of the baby and all those details about the operation.'

'Now you know why we came away,' said Pina. 'Once was enough. I know more about Caesareans than Caesar's mother.'

'What's Caesarean?' asked Chiara.

'That's the name of the operation where they cut out the baby if the mother cannot deliver it naturally,' said Lola.

'It's supposed to have been the way that Julius Caesar was born but they must have done it before him.'

'And now the fun begins,' said Lola meaningfully. 'This child is not going to have an easy time with Natty for her mother. Little Angel indeed... well, we shall see. But I need consolation from a bigger Angel. So let's see what I can have with my tea. Your millefeuille looks lovely,

Chiara. I might just have one of those. Can I have a taste of yours and then I'll decide.'

- Four -

Chiara and Pina returned home much sooner than they had anticipated because of the curtailed visit to Natalia's.

Chiara seemed fascinated by the details of Julius Caesar's birth and asked more questions than Pina could hope to be able to answer so she eventually stemmed the flood by telling her that she was sure that her father would be an expert on Roman emperors. Chiara awaited Remo's return with great anticipation.

He was surprised to find the two of them at home when he arrived, laden with bags and baskets. Chiara jumped up to greet him warmly and Pina just sighed at the sight of all those mushrooms which were going to need dealing with almost immediately, and the thought of all those creepy crawlies that were going to leave their homes in the funghi to crawl along her shelves and surfaces.

'But before we start,' she said, 'let's have a drink. Tea or Coffee, Remo?' And they all sat round the kitchen table together.

'These are for you, Chiara,' Remo said, producing a fair sized bag. 'I thought you could take some to school if there are too many for you.' And Chiara opened the bag to find a whole crop of gleaming, polished conkers, all waxy bright, some still half sleepily encased in their spiky shells.

'Chestnuts or conkers?' asked Pina. 'To eat, or to crack against each other?'

'No, these are for play only,' Remo explained. 'There were few edible chestnuts today. Maybe next time.'

'Why are they called conkers?' asked Chiara.

'No idea!' said Remo. 'Maybe because you use them in the game to beat your opponent…conquer?'

'Oh no!' laughed Chiara. 'That's so feeble.'

'Well, you do better!' said Remo.

'Pappa, you know about the Romans?'

'Do I?'

'Well Pina says you are an expert,' said Chiara seriously.

'So that must be true then,' said Remo with a look at Pina that said, *'Thanks for landing me in it!'*

'So, what can I tell you?'

'It's about Caesar,' said Chiara, 'and how he was born. Is it true they cut the baby out of his mother?'

'I believe so,' replied Remo, 'but I wasn't there so I don't know for sure.'

Oh Pappa, you are in a very funny mood tonight,' said Chiara laughing. 'No, I wondered, did it kill the mother to have the baby cut out like that?'

'Well, it didn't kill Natty, did it?' interrupted Pina. 'So it doesn't mean that one thing follows another automatically.'

'And it didn't kill Caesar's mother either,' rejoined Remo. 'If he was born like that. But memory says that Romans only cut the baby from a mother who was dead, to save the child, so I think there's a lot of confusion about the term they use today.'

'So,' continued Chiara, 'I was wondering. Was I born like that? Mamma didn't live after I was born and so...'

Pina saw the sudden tension in Remo's shoulders as he reacted to the unexpected question.

'No!' interjected Remo. 'Nothing like that. Your mother only lived for a couple of years after you were born. But you were born in a traditional way! Sorry to tell you, cara, you're not a descendent of the Caesars but if I don't behave myself, I may finish up like one of them.' And as he spoke he shifted out of his chair and reached for a bag of mushrooms and in so doing, he concealed his face and obscured his reaction. Not that Chiara noticed, but Pina was always on a knife's edge at such times.

'What do you mean?' asked Chiara, neatly diverted from her train of thought by her father's quick thinking.

'Well, it's said,' Remo replied with a solemn look, 'that the emperor Claudius loved mushrooms and that when his wife got tired of him, she slipped some poisoned mushrooms onto his plate with the ones he liked.'

'So, watch out!' Pina joined in, ensuring that the diversion was carried through. 'If I get too fed up with drying all these *porcini*, I may just slip in a few of my own.'

'Do you keep poisoned mushrooms?' asked Chiara, wide eyed at this unexpected statement.

'Well, I would have to, wouldn't I?' replied Pina. 'After all I am a step-mother, and we all know what a reputation they have!'

'But only in stories,' said Chiara, 'and we don't live in stories but in the real world.'

'So you think you've been in the real world today at Natty's?' said Pina. 'If that wasn't something out of a fairy tale, I don't know what is!'

And between them, Chiara and Pina regaled Remo with an account of their visit.

'It sounds like a film,' said Remo, 'with Natty in the starring role!'

'Only not in black and white,' said Pina.

'No, in full colour,' added Chiara, 'and most of it PINK!!'

Three Queens

The group of parents who gathered outside the railings on Duncan Terrace was quiet and sombre. By some sort of unspoken agreement they had come together earlier than usual, driven by an inexplicable communal need to be there waiting the moment that their children appeared at the close of the School day. They simply nodded at each other today. There was no attempt to exchange the usual small talk that passed the time between their arrival and the ringing of the hand bell within the building. Their unspoken agreement not to speak to each other was almost as if they feared that by speaking they would not hear the bell. It was foolish and yet though none of them said anything, if they had, they would have been surprised at how many of them were experiencing exactly the same feeling.

When the hand bell sounded, there was suddenly a marked concentration on the door and as it opened to release the children, there was a palpable sigh of relief and a movement to put arms round their precious offspring. The children's chatter was more subdued than usual until one young voice was heard above the rest.

'Is it true, mummy? Is the king really dead?' At which point, after a moment of uncertainty, conversation erupted between mothers and children.

Perhaps it was a sense of relief that the children had been told at school and so they had been spared trying to explain this collectively significant occurrence. Perhaps it was the realisation that what they had heard from the radio and from early newspaper vendors in the street, who hawked their news sheets by intoning the leading headline of the day, was really true.

The king was dead.

When Chiara eventually appeared on the steps, Pina was ready with a similar embrace to those offered by the other mothers and Chiara happily settled under the crook of her arm for the walk home. Nothing was said and there were no stops on the way. Traffic down the City Road seemed as usual and the walk past Alice Owens, down the narrow passage into Rosebery Avenue was as quiet as ever. The Water Board and Sadler's Wells showed no signs of anything different and yet, as the buses passed them, they seemed slower and more sombre than usual and people going to and fro seemed more wrapped up in themselves and reluctant to meet the gaze of any passersby.

It was only once they had reached the house, and had gone in to find Remo waiting by the stove with a kettle almost ready to boil, that Chiara realised that it was Pina who had met her today, not her father as was usual. She hadn't registered this fact as anything out of the ordinary until now when she saw her parents in a roles reversed situation.

'You'll miss Mrs Dale, if you don't turn on the radio,' said Chiara to Pina.

'Not today,' replied Pina. 'Radio's quiet today.'

'Because of the king?' asked Chiara.

'Yes, cara, it's a mark of respect.'

'What did he die of?' asked Chiara.

'Too early to say,' replied Remo, making the tea.

'But it's likely to be from smoking too much. Everyone knows what a heavy smoker he was. All that stress of becoming king so suddenly and so unprepared.'

'It was the old queen who pushed him into it,' added Pina. 'She was determined not to have her first son as a king with...erm...that American as his wife...' And she trailed off, not wanting to become embroiled in the whys and wherefores of the abdication, the divorced woman and adultery.

'We heard the story of the death of King Arthur this afternoon,' said Chiara. 'Instead of reading ourselves, Sister read it out to us. But I don't understand something...'

Pina and Remo waited.

'Did King Arthur die or not? The story says he was taken away on a barge and that one day he'll return when his country needs him. How can he return if he's dead, or how could he have stayed alive all those years? What's really the truth?' And she paused, looking earnestly from one adult to the other and waiting for the answer from one or other to be offered.

'Well,' began Pina, 'he may not have died then but have fallen into a deathlike sleep so that he can be woken up again one day.' She paused, waiting to see if her words were going to be sufficient.

'But surely his country needed him when we were at war?' asked Chiara. 'Has he been back then at sometime between then and now? Why didn't anyone recognise him?'

'We don't know,' Remo interrupted. 'We cannot know for sure. Maybe the story means that the spirit of King Arthur comes back into his people when they need it…that they find courage to fight on and win.'

Chiara pondered and nodded. 'Yes, that's a good idea,' she said.

'But what happened to the three queens who were with him? Did they die or come back as well?'

'Three queens?' asked Pina. 'I don't remember anything about them.'

'Yes,' said Chiara, 'one was his wicked sister and the other two didn't have names, they were just queens in the story.'

'Why was his wicked sister with him?' asked Remo, puzzled and intrigued now by the imagery of the story.

'Sister said it was for her to make her peace with him, a sort of confession before he died or else she wouldn't have had the chance to say sorry for all the harm she did. Sister says that's like confession for us when we go and tell the priest our sins and he forgives us.'

'No, cara, that's not quite right,' said Pina gently. 'We say what we've done wrong in front of the priest but we're really talking to God and He forgives us. The priest is there just to tell us that God is listening and forgives us. It's to reassure us.'

'So we don't need a priest really?' said Chiara. 'We can just talk to God directly?'

'Of course,' said Remo, 'but sometimes a priest helps you to work out what's wrong in your life and can suggest how to make it better. Well that's how it's been for me.' And he glanced quickly and almost slyly at Pina as he said this. She caught the glance and her eyes smiled at him.

'So,' continued Chiara, obliviously, 'we don't really need to go to confession.'

'*Need* might be the wrong word,' said Pina. 'We should make it a habit to go as it's a good habit and can help us to balance all the bad habits we develop as we get older.'

'Do you go to confession, Pina?' asked Chiara directly and looking straight at her.

'Not that often,' replied Pina. 'But I do go and have a chat with Fr Martyn and then if he thinks there's a need he gives me a blessing which is less formal a way but just as good. But for now, young lady, it's confession as usual for you when school arranges it.'

'Pina?' asked Chiara after a little more thought.

'Yes, cara.'

'About the three queens...'

'Yes, Chiara.'

'The king who's dead...he'll have three queens round him too, won't he?'

'I suppose you're right,' said Pina, taken by surprise. 'His mother, his wife and his daughter, who became queen as soon as he died. Three queens.'

'Do you think the dead king could have been King Arthur coming back to save his country when it needed him?' Chiara asked earnestly.

'That might just be a little fanciful,' her father said.

'But there are three queens around him too.'

'Yes, cara,' replied Pina quickly, 'but one of them is not his wicked sister. So that's a good thing at least...Tea time, I think. So let's get the table cleared and ready.'

- Two -

The lying in state and then the funeral of the king filled the papers over the next week or so and Remo took Pina and Chiara to a news cinema so that they could watch the ceremonies on the newsreels as it was a significant moment in history and he wanted Chiara to remember it. But he had his own motives as well as he found that he had become intrigued by the imagery of the three queens. Pina and Chiara noticed that he was spending much more time than usual on his sketch pads as he worked on pictures which might eventually serve as templates for carvings or sculptures. His work although modern in style was not representing the historical scenes being played out before the people of London but was rather a contemporary interpretation of the stories of which Chiara had reminded him, the stories of the death of Arthur.

It was refreshing for him to be dealing with a theme other than religious but once he saw in a paper an iconic photograph of the three queens in their mourning clothes which were stirred by a breeze, and their generation grouping, his imagination took fire and he set to work not on King Arthur but on the three women who stood at the foot of the Cross, a very modern Crucifixion but with sorrow expressed through pose and stance and gesture rather than by facial expression, as the faces of all three women were concealed by veils.

Chiara and Pina were astonished at the ferocity with which he approached the subject and by the fact that his chosen medium for it was not his usual.

He set up a great easel in the studio and embarked on a large canvas.

The startling aspect of his Crucifixion was that only the bottom part of the cross was visible to one side of the picture. Not even the block on which the feet were supported could be seen. So, the emphasis was entirely on the grief and interaction of the three grieving women, and they were strongly based on the three queens from the funeral.

His palette was unusual as well as he experimented with sepia tones as if he were painting a photograph. And he worked with such speed that the whole was completed in days.

He took several photographs of the finished work, took the film to the developers and when the prints were returned, he set about sending them to several addresses abroad.

Pina took the letters to the post with a heavy heart as she knew that if any one of the churches in France, Spain or Italy replied positively, then that would mean a separation and she hated the family unit being broken up for any amount of time at all.

There was a trickle of correspondence from foreign parts. Enough to keep Chiara happy with the foreign stamps for her collection once Remo had opened them and read the contents. With his usual reserve however he made no comment about their substance until some three weeks later he brought a handful to the table at breakfast time one Saturday.

'There are just three replies of interest,' he began. 'One from a church in Spain, one from a gallery in Italy and one from a convent in the south of France.'

'Why don't you just paint two more versions of the same picture and satisfy them all,' said Chiara. 'Everyone would be happy then.'

'Except me,' added Pina suddenly and rather surprised at herself. 'If it meant three foreign trips instead of just one.'

'Well,' said Remo, reacting inwardly but not outwardly to the ferocity of Pina's response, 'I wouldn't have to go to the gallery in Italy. They say that they would be happy to pay the expenses of packing and posting. But the church and the convent both include travelling expenses and say that they would expect me to attend the hanging of the picture and its blessing. However, they are also offering a reliably larger sum. The gallery offers a minimum payment and then a percentage of what it sells for when on display. So, if it doesn't sell, I get a lump sum anyway but maybe nothing else in the long run. Not an easy decision then to make.'

'We can help you with that,' said Chiara unexpectedly. 'I have an idea. We will play Newmarket tonight when Zia Lola comes with Franca and Rosa.'

'I don't see how that will help,' said Remo intrigued and smiling.

'I need to work it out a bit more in my head,' said Chiara, 'but you'll see. I think it will work and by tonight your decision will be made…by three queens!'

Pina just shrugged her shoulders and looked baffled but Chiara was up quickly after breakfast and took the cards from the drawer where they were kept.

- Three -

After supper that evening, the whole family was gathered round the big kitchen table as usual. And when it was discussed what game they would play that night, Chiara spoke up. 'If no one minds, can we have at least one game of Newmarket only with slightly different rules tonight? I'd like there to be just three Kings not four set out. On the back of each one I've made small pencil marks, easy to rub out later. On this piece of paper I've written the names of the Convent, the Church and the Gallery with 1, 2 and 3 by them. I left out the King of Spades. I never like the Queen of Spades. So we have just Hearts, Diamonds and Clubs. We play as usual, working the suits out until there is only one King left. Then we look and see what number is on the reverse. And the decision is made. How does that sound?'

Astonished, Pina and Remo nodded quietly while Lola and the girls who had heard all about the painting and the dilemma were happy to go along with it especially as the stakes of a penny on a card and a penny in the kitty were to be observed as usual, so there would still be the thrill of a winner for one or the other or more likely, both.

And so the cards were dealt out and the game with its twists and turns and thrills and frustrations was played out.

First to fall was the Hearts Queen who got to her King and made Lola richer by 4 pence. Then Clubs fell, this time to Rosa, and that left Diamonds. It was clear then that whatever was written on the back of Diamonds was going to be the decision. But the game was played as usual, with the working out of the Spades Queen who had no King to go to so that trail was dead. And all concentration was now on Diamonds.

Who was holding the Queen anyway? Everyone had played this well enough and often enough to know not to reveal so that there was an element of surprise. And indeed there was, as it was Lola who triumphed a second time. But she reached the kitty and the King was left unclaimed by a Queen.

'So who had the Queen?' asked Pina.

'I have her,' said Remo. 'But I couldn't play her.'

'What a lucky hand you had!' exclaimed Pina who had had a miserable selection of cards throughout.

'So, we shall have to start again,' said Chiara, now a little anxiously as she scooped up the cards and replaced the Kings.

The cards were shuffled. The pennies were laid again on Kings of choice and in the kitty and then the cards were dealt. Everyone glanced at the others' faces to see if they could spot a flicker of delight on them. They had all learnt the art of keeping their faces without expression, though Chiara thought she saw Franca twisting a little in her seat and that might mean that she had a good hand.

The Queen of Hearts soon claimed her King this time and Pina was rewarded for her patience, but then Rosa swept in with both the kitty and the Queen of Clubs and once again there was a lonely King without his Queen, left on the table.

A third hand was dealt, and now there was tension. Chiara could feel how the other players were all anxious to know which of the Queens would win. Rosa claimed the Clubs King with her card, and so the battle was between the Diamond and the Hearts Queens as to which would be left to the last. Franca claimed the Diamond King with her Queen and there were few cards left.

Would the kitty be claimed and once again leave a King without his Queen?

There was a short swift run, a flurry of cards from Pina's hand. And suddenly, she laid down the Queen of Hearts and revealed that that had been the last card in her hand.

Everyone sighed. 'Well done!'

As the Queen was laid on the King, Pina picked up the cards and revealed that there were three small dots on the back.

Chiara handed over the paper to her father.

'So, Pappa, tell us all which it is to be.'

'The Gallery in Florence,' he said.

And Pina breathed a sigh, though she tried to conceal it.

Chiara noticed. 'Are you sure you're happy with that?' she said. 'We could always play it out again, three times and take the best of three.'

'No,' said Remo, 'I'll abide by that and take it as it comes. It looks as if I'll be around all summer, if that's alright with you.'

Chiara beamed.

'I think we'll cope,' she said, not daring to look at Pina.

'So, another game then. This time with all four Kings.'

'Yes please,' said Chiara. 'But first I must rub out the pencil marks or we'll know what the cards are when they are being dealt in other games.'

And she hastily gathered up the Queens and Kings from the table and took them off to one side, and made very certain that the pencil marks were all rubbed out. She glanced quickly at the others as she did so but no one was taking any notice. If they had, they might have seen that there were three dots to be erased from all three Kings... but the art of a prestidigitator is to conceal his trickery.

The Queen of Hearts smiled on Chiara that evening.

Smog

- One -

'Could you make sure all the windows upstairs are tightly closed, Chiara,' called Pina from the kitchen. 'I don't want that vile stuff in the house if we can avoid it.'

'It's much worse than usual,' said Chiara. 'I can't see across the street. Should we set off earlier than usual for school?'

'I'm not sure about school today,' replied Pina as Chiara reappeared in the kitchen. 'I don't think it's very sensible to go out across the roads. The nuns will be fine as they only live next door but I don't know how many children will make the effort to get there. They've got to get home again when it's getting darker as well. Hmm. Not at all sensible to be out. I think we'll stay put for today. We don't need shopping and it's bound to have cleared a bit by tomorrow. I wonder if the milkman will deliver.'

'We have enough milk even if he doesn't. Pappa isn't here and won't need his milky coffee.'

'He's not due back until Sunday evening,' said Pina. 'I wonder how widespread this is. Will it affect the ferries? And the trains? We should keep the radio on for bulletins.'

'Oh good,' said Chiara. 'That means I can hear *Music while you work* and *Mrs Dale* today. I only get to hear them in the holidays or when I'm not well.'

'And *Workers' Playtime*,' added Pina. 'We'll have that on at lunch time.'

They settled into the cosiness of being at home and they indulged themselves in piling on coal as the temperatures were unusually chilly.

Chiara practised some school exercises from the books she had brought home for homework and then went downstairs to finish off painting some statues, and Pina went about her usual Friday chores, preparing a special cake as well as her usual cooking for the weekend which was to be spent at her sister's, though that might have to be rethought.

As the two busied themselves within, the density of the atmosphere outside thickened. The street lamps were not extinguished but left burning. The lamplighters did not attempt their usual rounds but the meagre gleam of gaslight did nothing to penetrate the murkiness and its only use was to show those attempting to walk along a pavement where they might expect to find a lamppost and avoid bumping into it.

By midmorning when they had decided to meet for biscuits and *Mrs Dale's Diary*, the house was totally cut off from anywhere else. Nothing could be seen from the windows, save the gleam of gas light. More eerily, nothing could be heard. The radio told them that London was in the grip of smog.

What's that?' asked Chiara. 'Not fog?'

'Not just fog but smoke as well,' said Pina, 'and we're causing it with our fires blazing away. It's the smoke that can't escape into the atmosphere and is trapped. We are wrapped in it. Best to keep everything closed tight. Breathing it in would be very bad for the chest.'

'Just as well Pappa's not here,' said Chiara. 'He has trouble with chestiness in winter, doesn't he?'

'Yes,' said Pina. 'It was caused by him smoking so much in Italy before he came here. He gave up more or less once he settled here with you and the colder air here made him breathless more easily. That's what he says anyway and it's good to be in a house where no one smokes except visitors. Fr Martyn is the worst and…'

'I know,' said Chiara. 'Everything smells of smoke after he's gone. Sometimes for days. But everyone smokes,' she added. 'Why didn't you?'

'Well I did when I was in London. So did Lola and she used to like those American cigarettes that her husband had. And then, when I went back to Italy to look after my family, I stopped. Well it was hard to get cigarettes over there in the village and I just grew out of the habit and Lola said she only liked the American fags so she gave up over here once the supply stopped. Mind you, she'll often have one at Natty's when she goes. Natty didn't stop. She didn't even stop when she had the baby. One after another in front of the telly in the evening. Not so bad when you girls are there for tea or to watch TV. But usually she has far too many and her cough is really bad so she should know better.'

'What if this smog is really all the smoke from cigarettes that can't escape into the atmosphere,' asked Chiara. 'I can see all those people endlessly smoking and their smoke being trapped and…'

'Oh Chiara, you and your fancy,' said Pina. 'I think it would take a lot of cigarette smoke to cause this thickness of fog.'

'Yes, but just think. If we are now looking at smoke that can't escape and it smells so bad and makes us cough and feel ill, what must the smoke from cigarettes do when it gets trapped inside your body?'

'Enough!' said Pina. 'Time for Mrs Dale. I bet it's not foggy at all in Parkwood Hill today.'

Chiara looked puzzled. 'But surely it must be, if it's foggy everywhere in London as the radio says. So why…?'

But the sound of the harp heralding the opening of the Diary put paid to any further discussion.

'Of course,' thought Chiara to herself, 'that is a repeat of yesterday's episode and it wasn't so bad then.'

And her own logic satisfied her need to question further as she became involved in the daily doings of the Dales and wondered whether Mrs Freeman's cat would make an appearance or that frightful but entertaining Mrs Mountford.

There was no lifting of gloom as the day progressed and although darkness fell, there was little difference in the level of light outside by the time that the afternoon episode of Mrs Dale was broadcast but by that time Chiara seemed to have forgotten her morning's preoccupation with weather conditions in Parkwood Hill.

- Two -

Saturday morning dawned but the rosy fingers of Aurora made no impact on the grey green yellow swirls outside the house.

'I'm going to have to go and do some shopping,' Pina said. 'I'll just go down Exmouth Street as far as Woolies. I need to pop into the butcher's but I won't be gone long.'

'You're not going alone,' said Chiara. 'It's not sensible. I'm coming with you and we can guide each other along the railings and over the roads.'

'No, not at all,' said Pina.

'Yes,' replied Chiara with determination. 'I'll come too. And we'll make face masks so as not to breathe in too much nastiness. We can tie them on with a scarf or one of Pappa's ties that he hardly uses.'

Pina reflected as she got together her basket and string bag. 'Very well. I give in. You do the masks. You're right. I'll be pleased to have company and you won't be fretting about me while I'm out.'

The minute that they had shut the door behind them, Pina knew that they had made the right decision to go together. Their faces were almost totally covered in the masks Chiara had made from wetted handkerchiefs, hand towels and scarves. It meant that they couldn't speak but their noses and mouths were protected. They held tightly to each other's arms and made a cautious way along the street close to the railings of the basements. There was no traffic so crossing the few short roads to the start of the market presented no problems. Each side of the market glowed as shopkeepers tried to brighten the street. Stall holders had not attempted to set up their wares so the street was clear. They kept to the right hand side and Pina allowed Chiara a few minutes to glance in the windows of Solly's, the toy shop. The door was closed against the smog but it was clear that the toy seller was trying to arrange his window display for Christmas. They reached almost the end of the street opposite Holy Redeemer Church and Pina pushed open the door of the butcher's. The shop was well lit and the sawdust on the floor made it feel somehow brighter. A boy of about Chiara's age was being served.

'Won't be long, Mrs R,' called out the lady at the counter, giving Pina and Chiara time to untie their masks so that they could speak.

'Have you come all this way on your own?' the lady asked the boy.

'No, my Dad's with me. He's popped into Woolworth's and told me to wait here for him. He said to collect the order.'

'Yes, here it is. Marked as usual with your Grandma's name. Funny how we never changed that even after your mother got married and your gran died. It's all paid for. Don't drop it now.' And she handed over two well wrapped parcels of white paper.

As the boy turned from the counter, Chiara said, 'I thought it was you, Tonio. We miss you at school.'

'Hello, Chiara. I'm pleased to see you. I'm at a different school now. The one next to the church.'

'We all wondered where you went. Do you like the new school?'

'Well, it's alright, I suppose. But I'm in the top class and everyone is older than me and knows more than me and there are lots more people than at the convent.'

As the children chattered, Pina did her shopping then she said, 'Chiara, if you wait here with your friend, I'll just pop over to Higgens' for some eggs and cheese and things, then we'll start back. Is that all right with you, Gladys?' she asked. 'If the children stay here for a short while?'

'No problem, Mrs R,' replied good natured Gladys.

Pina didn't bother to retie the mask but just held it over her face as she crossed the street.

'Our classrooms are bigger,' said Tonio, 'but we move our places quite often and I don't like that. Sometimes I have to sit next to someone I don't like much. One boy smells really bad. It's horrible having to sit next to him.'

'Maybe his family is really poor,' said Chiara, 'and can't look after him properly. We're lucky, you don't have brothers and sisters, and nor do I. It makes a difference. I know when I'm with my cousins.'

'Me too. My Zia has a baby now and everyone is always concentrating round her. Even my mum is always round there these days as my Zia is having trouble.'

'Your Zia…' said Chiara, 'she's Natty, my mum's friend, isn't she?'

'Yes,' replied Tonio, 'she's my dad's sister, you know. We go round every week for a bath and to watch TV. Usually on a Friday…but my mum's there almost every night these days.'

'There you are,' said Chiara. ' You can have a bath but not everyone is so lucky.'

'I'll think about that when I have to sit next to that boy again…oh, here's my Dad now.'

And suddenly in the shop doorway there appeared a muffled shape. He pushed the door open and nodded to the boy.

'Coming?'

'Yes Dad.'

'Thanks for keeping an eye, Glad,' said Tonio's father, and just at that moment, Pina reappeared. She entered the cluttered doorway and started to replace the mask.

'So, can we go and watch the buses, Dad?' asked Tonio.

'OK, just to the corner of Mt Pleasant and then back home or your mother will have a go at me!'

'Oh Pina, can we go with them,' asked Chiara, 'just to the end of the market?'

'Do you mind?' said Pina, who was no less caught up in the mystery of this unshifting fog than the children.

'Not at all. If we keep together with the kids between us, we'll be fine. There's no one about.'

Waving to Gladys and the butcher who had emerged from the back cold room to see his brave customers, the little band set out, closing the shop door tightly behind them, they walked across the narrow street just the few steps to the corner of Farringdon Road. There they stood in silence, as if waiting for some great procession. They stood in silence, huddled against each other and saw nothing but the swirling thickness.

And then, from the distance beyond the Post Office, a tiny light appeared high up, and the sound of a distant rumble. They were aware of some great shape looming and lumbering towards them. Not exactly a shape, just one high panel of light and below it a duller oblong over which the greyness danced. In the upper brightness the figures 38 were visible and beneath, obscured place names, partly familiar, a bit illegible, places which would be visited by this monster whose redness had drained from its body as it steadfastly pursued its hazardous journey. It paused at the warning traffic lights, and then slowly with a grinding of internal organs, it thrust forward almost reluctantly, gasping at the effort and revealing bands of light along its sides from upper and lower windows against which dim silhouettes of passengers' heads could be discerned. It passed by them slowly and the space it had filled for a brief moment was seized once more by the overactive grey-green sludge of the disturbed atmosphere.

The boy and his father had only handkerchiefs over their faces and the boy was starting to cough, so with a bow and a wave of the hand to the ladies, father and son moved away across the Avenue towards Marshall's the grocers on the corner. But they were gone from sight before they had even half crossed the road.

Pina put her arm round Chiara's shoulder and they retrod the length of the market back home in the all enveloping silence.

When they reached home and were settled comfortably by the fire, Chiara said, 'Pina, do you remember that book I had for Christmas about little people...the hobbits?'

'I remember reading some of it to you but you said it wasn't very good for girls.'

'Well that's true,' replied Chiara, 'but I remembered when we were watching that bus, that there's a dragon in that book called Smaug. I think we've seen him today. It was a bit scary.'

- Three -

They saw nobody for the rest of the day. On Sunday morning they wrapped their faces again and ventured out the short distance to Mass which was very poorly attended.

Pina's anxiety as afternoon on the clock dwindled into evening became more difficult to stifle. There was no change in the outside world. Without the radio there would have been isolation so profound as to make one fear for one's sanity but the constant regularity of familiar voices and music bred an air of comfort and security amid the uncertainty of what was now unfamiliar London just over the threshold.

Sunday evening came and the time for bed arrived. Pina and Chiara ate their meal almost in silence, feigning close attention to the evening's radio programmes, neither wanting to raise the question that they each knew the other could not answer.

'What about…' Chiara started with a slight pause, 'school tomorrow?'

'Don't think about it!' Pina replied, realising that by keeping Chiara at home with her, her loneliness and anxiety would be easier to bear.

'Now, off to bed and prayers and a little read and I'll come in later and tuck you up.'

Monday came and went and there was no change, in any aspect of the situation. You could not see your hand in front of your face. A neighbour knocked at the door and startled Pina by the noise from outside her enclosed world. But it was only to ask if she was alright and to tell her that at Sadler's Wells they had cancelled the opera after one act as the smog so filled the auditorium that the stage was barely visible.

Tuesday, suddenly, a change.

Pina still took no chances and kept Chiara at home, but by the afternoon it was obvious that the clouds of plague were passing into another atmosphere and there was light.

So by Wednesday, it was school as usual.

Pina returned from shopping after she had taken Chiara to school. She had resisted the offer of joining some of the other mothers for a cup of tea and a chat and had hardly set down her bags and unpacked the shopping when there was a loud banging on the front door knocker.

She rushed down, her heart full of hopeful anticipation, flung the door open and saw before her on the doorstep, the caped and helmeted figure of a man in blue.

It was a policeman.

'Mrs Romani?'

'Yes.'

'Don't be anxious. I have some news for you.'

'My husband?'

'Yes. He's in hospital.'

'What? Where? What's happened? Oh sorry, please, come in.' And Pina ushered the policemen into the kitchen, while her heart and breath settled down from that momentary fear of the worst news possible to the curiosity of what had happened and what needed to be done and how bad it was and all those other rapid blasts of thought half-formed that zigzag through the brain when something unexpected occurs.

'Please, sit down,' she said.

'We have had a lot of trouble with this weather,' said the policeman, removing his helmet so that he looked less ferocious and official and much more of a human being. 'This is why it's taken so long to get to you. Your husband was taken into St George's hospital on Monday. He collapsed trying to find a bus at Victoria station. It's his chest. They took him into hospital but there have been so many similar cases that it's been difficult to get men out to notify families about what has happened. He had identification on him fortunately. A lot of people don't. I'm afraid I can't tell you much more. We only got the call at the station this morning and I tried earlier but you were out.'

'Yes, taking my daughter to school,' Pina said. 'What can I say? Thank you, officer. Can I offer you a cup of tea?'

'Better not,' he replied, 'as I've a few more calls to make. More people like you to put out of their misery! And then must get back to the station.'

And he stood up to go, resettled his helmet into place on his head, adjusting the chin strap and made his way down to the door.

Pina opened it for him, waved him off from the step and then came back indoors, pushing the door shut.

The she just slumped onto the floor, sobbing with the release of all the tension of uncertainty and with the relief.

She soon gathered herself together, wiped away her tears and started to think. There was plenty of time before she would need to collect Chiara, but what would she have to do…what if when…what? She pushed the unanswerables aside and got herself ready as speedily as she could.

She didn't have to wait long for a bus to Hyde Park Corner and the journey through the familiar places of Central London was reassuring and calming. A few hours later she made the return journey but she was still alone.

When Chiara came out of school, she ran into the welcoming arms of Pina who was smiling.

'He's home then!' she exclaimed. 'Pappa's back!'

'Not exactly, cara,' said Pina. 'He won't be back for a few days but we'll see him sooner.'

And as they walked slowly back along Duncan Terrace, Pina explained calmly and matter of factly what had happened.

'So we were right,' said Chiara. 'He has a weak chest from smoking.'

'Yes,' said Pina, 'and the thickness of the smog and long journey back from Italy through France just weakened him. They say he'll be fine but won't let him home until they are sure. So we'll go and see him this evening. Visiting hours are a bit later. We'll have our tea first and then try to get there for opening so long as the traffic isn't too bad. At least policemen won't be guiding the bus with flares. That's what happened over the last couple of days, so the conductor told me this morning. Anyway, no need for us to worry. We'll be bringing him home soon. I just need to take him some clean pyjamas and a dressing gown.'

'And his slippers,' added Chiara. 'Then he'll really feel at home. And I'll take him my book about the hobbits to read, and then he'll know all about the evils of Smaug.'

The Empire

- One -

It was impossible not to be fascinated by the blue kettle. It was fixed quite high over the cafe that was named after it. How the steam was channeled through and out of the kettle's spout was a constant source of wonder to all who passed through these side streets at the Angel, Islington. It was so much a part of the ambiance of the place that when the steam failed to appear, there was cause for consternation and conversation.

Lunches at the Convent School in Duncan Terrace were not cooked on the premises. For many years they had been prepared in a private house some streets away, packed into tins which slotted onto each other and were then secured tightly by a leather strap and collected towards the end of morning school by children from the top class. It was a charmingly old fashioned method of providing a hot meal for children at the school but the time came when things had to change and it was decided to investigate whether the Blue Kettle cafe might be the best business to take over this responsibility. It delighted the children to know that their lunches would be coming from this iconic landmark in the area and the numbers of those having lunch at the school rose in anticipation of the suggested change.

Chiara's inquisitive nature and persuasive approach to whatever intrigued her had eventually led to Pina taking her into the cafe for a treat and after one or two visits, the child was confident enough to persuade the owners to reveal the secret workings of the mystery which she promised never to divulge.

Satisfied with her success, Chiara now turned her attention to another puzzling attraction of her little world, the flea-pit cinema on the main road which was clearly a relic of grander times but which was now sorely neglected.

The frontage still bore all the architectural decorations of its glory days, even though the grime of traffic and the passage of wartime had coated the facade in dirt and decay, and its future, even as a cheap cinema did not look assured.

The walls displayed torn posters with long faded colours that showed it had once served as a music hall even though its much more famous sister was still flourishing successfully just down the road on the Green.

Chiara knew little of Music Hall. Pina, only a little more, as it was not part of the background of entertainment which Italians generally attended. But there was something about the look of the old building that attracted Chiara's interest and once this was sparked, it was hard to suppress it.

'Pina?'

'Yes, Chiara.'

'Why is it called Music Hall?'

'Do you mean the building we pass?'

'Well, yes, I suppose so. It doesn't look like a hall. We have a school hall which we call the Salle. Is it big like that inside with tables and benches?'

'No, I don't think so. I believe it has rows of seats as in a theatre or cinema. But I've never been in to either of the two near us. We could go to Collins, one day, I suppose if the people on the bill sound reasonable.'

'What do they do then if it's not plays or films? Is it like a school concert with songs and a piano?'

'Well there is music, of course, but also acrobats and dancers and people telling jokes like on the radio but I think it's mainly for grown-ups not really for children.'

'Why not? I like some of the music on the radio.'

'Yes, well it's not serious music generally.'

'You mean it's like *Children's Favourites*?'

'Well, yes, but more grown-up.'

'Pina?'

'Yes, Chiara.'

'Does grown-up mean it's something rude?'

'Well, darling, you are on the right lines, that's why we would have to see who is performing. Now if it's Gert and Daisy, we would be fine but some of the men tell jokes that we wouldn't understand and wouldn't be suitable.'

'So could we go to the little Music Hall that's a cinema instead? I would love to see inside.'

'That's possible. I'll keep an eye on the films they show and choose something we might both like. Who knows, we might even get your father to come along too.'

There wasn't long to wait before something suitable for a family appeared on the bill boards and the Romani family made its way with some excitement one Saturday afternoon to the box office of the Islington Empire.

They arrived early and had plenty of time in which to view the interior of the old theatre. It was shabby and faded but had drawn quite a good crowd in for the afternoon showing of a film calculated to appeal to most elements in a family. But Chiara was less interested in the show that would soon appear on the screen than in the building itself. Great heavy curtains hung across the proscenium masking the screen and the feel was of a theatre rather than a cinema.

Chiara absorbed the atmosphere and wrinkled her nose a little.

'Pina?'

'Yes, cara.'

'Can you smell something funny?'

Pina sniffed the air. Yes there was mustiness from the not very well cleaned seats and carpet…a staleness. But…

'No, not that,' said Chiara. 'That's just because there's not much fresh air in here. No, I mean something else.'

'Well, don't let it worry you,' said Remo, and look the lights are going down so we'll be starting soon.'

'I know,' said Chiara, preoccupied, 'it's a smell of something burnt. Not burning. But burnt.'

'Not now, Chiara,' said her father. 'Later…later.'

And the curtains swung back to reveal the screen as music filled the auditorium and the excited chatter of the audience died down as the first images appeared before them. The News.

The lights went up again after a few advertisements had followed the newsreel and the usherettes appeared in the aisles with their little trays of ice creams hung round their necks.

'I need to go to the toilet,' said Chiara suddenly.

'Shall I come with you,' asked Pina, who had visited before the performance started.

'No, I saw where they are,' said Chiara. 'I'll be fine'.

'Don't be long,' said her father. 'The main film will start in five minutes or so.'

But Chiara had already darted off.

They were sitting in the stalls and the toilets were certainly on that level but suddenly Pina caught sight of Chiara on the first floor, making her way along in the direction of one of the boxes that overlooked the stage.

'Look, Remo,' she said, tapping his arm, 'What's she up to?'

'Say nothing,' Remo replied. 'Let her have her adventure. It's quite safe here.'

And just as the lights dimmed again, Chiara reappeared and settled into her seat with a sigh of satisfaction and a secret smile.

The films seemed to have made much less of an impression on Chiara than the cinema itself and over the rest of the weekend she could not stop talking about it.

'Let's see what we can find out next week,' suggested Pina.

'The library is bound to have something about it.'

- Two -

So after school Chiara was in a great hurry to get home with Remo, and she and Pina swiftly set off towards Rosebery Avenue to the edge of Wilmington Square where the newly built Treasure Island Library was situated.

It was always a treat to go there, as the Library was dedicated to books for children and Chiara was well known to the librarians but today she was a little less sure than usual and didn't quite know what to ask or how to ask it, and when Pina tried on her behalf to explain, the librarians shook their heads.

'It's not really the sort of information that we keep here but you are bound to find something in the main library, over the road.'

'But I'm not allowed to go there yet,' said Chiara.

'But I am,' replied Pina with a smile, 'so come on, let's strike while the iron is hot.'

And thanking the lady at the desk for her help, they walked across Rosebery Avenue to the grand old building just off the end of Exmouth Street Market where the steps led up to what seemed like very serious doors to Chiara. She had never actually been into this library before and was full of excitement and wonder at the feel of the place with its shining glass and polished brass.

When they reached the desk, Pina addressed the librarian working there at his box of index cards and stamps.

'My daughter…' she began. And as she spoke she felt the still quite unfamiliar and delightful thrill of having a child whom she could think of as her own. 'My daughter has been sent to you from Treasure Island and I'll leave it to her to explain what she would like to ask you.'

Chiara looked a little taken aback by the need to find the right words suddenly, but seizing her chance she began. 'I would like to know the history of the Empire.'

The librarian was certainly surprised.

'Erm, that's quite a big subject,' he replied. 'We need a starting point...British or Roman?'

'Well, it's a cinema now,' Chiara continued, 'but I think it was once a theatre.'

The librarian smiled with some relief.

'Oh I see,' he replied, 'and which Empire did you have in mind?'

'The one at the Angel,' said Chiara.

Well, you'll need to see our expert on local matters,' said the librarian. 'I don't know if he is in today but you'll find someone in the Archive reference section who can tell you. It's just along there,' he said, pointing. 'Good luck with your search. You'll find he's very helpful.'

'Thank you,' they both said in unison as they made their way along. But disappointment awaited them.

'I'm afraid it's the archivist's day off,' said a young girl. 'He usually takes Monday off to have a long weekend and it's better if you see him as it's not really my area of knowledge. What I can do for you though is show you where to find books on the area. You're welcome to look through those on your own. We are very proud here to have been the first Library to allow people to browse through our collection of books without the help of a librarian, so you are very welcome to do so. And I'll leave a note for him when he returns tomorrow so that he'll be prepared when you come back later in the week, if that's alright.'

'Oh thank you so much,' said Chiara, and turning to Pina, asked, 'Will it be alright to come after school tomorrow?'

'Of course, Chiara. Tomorrow or the next day. The books won't run away and maybe we should give the man a chance to catch his breath when he comes back to work before making a nuisance of ourselves.'

'Oh you won't be a nuisance,' said the girl. 'He loves the area and knows all about its history so he'll be delighted to talk to you. But meantime, this is the best I can do to show you where things are kept. It would be better if you waited for him though and I'll just write a note and leave it on his desk if you give me your names.'

'Let's wait,' said Chiara, rather taking Pina by surprise at her sudden patience. 'It'll be something to look forward to later in the week.'

And thanking the young girl and with a wave to the helpful librarian at the main desk, they made their way home to their tea.

When they returned a couple of days later, they found only an elderly man on duty in the archive. Neat and thin, he peered at Pina over the top of his glasses in a way one expects of proper gentleman librarians. Had he been female, then you might have expected the glasses to have been strung around the neck on a chain and lifted to the eyes when appropriate, but as it was, the male convention gave him just the right appearance of competence, authority and kindliness that one looks for in a person in this position.

'I believe,' Pina began, 'that your assistant may have left you a note about…'

'Theatres? Ah yes, come this way please, Mrs Romani, and bring your daughter too if she's interested, otherwise…'

'Erm, actually,' Pina interjected, 'it's my daughter who is the one with the interest.'

'Oh' said the gentleman, totally taken aback. And then with a huge beam of a smile, he extended his hand to Chiara.

'A fellow enthusiast. You are starting young. I can't tell you how pleased I am to welcome you. Let's see what we can do for you…' And he opened a door behind him that led into his office and pulled round a couple of chairs for them.

'So,' he said, 'where to begin?'

And taking out from a cardboard box a selection of old postcards, he began a very comprehensive but simple account of the history of the little Islington theatre.

Chiara was particularly enthralled by the story of its history when it was called The Philharmonic and The Grand and when she heard how it had been burnt out, she turned to Pina with a very knowing look.

For the moment, Pina was uncomprehending and then she remembered what Chiara had said on first entering the cinema.

'That smell. That strange smell. You said it was like burning,' said Pina.

'Yes,' Chiara replied, 'but it was so far back, so long ago.'

'So,' said the archivist when he had laid out everything before them, 'are you ready?'

'For what?' asked Chiara and Pina, almost in unison.

From a wide shelf under his desk, the librarian produced a folder. 'These are newspapers,' he said, 'from the heyday of the theatre and I thought you might like to see this one in particular.'

He opened the folder to reveal a paper called The Graphic. In the middle of the front page was an etching of a woman's face.

'I thought this might interest you as she was a local girl who made her name here.'

'What was her name?' asked Chiara.

'Emily,' he replied, 'Emily Soldene and from very humble roots she travelled the world and was a great star in America and Australia but like you, her origins were from round here. Born and bred locally, Star of the Philly in the days of Queen Victoria. She had the gentry making their way from the West End all the way to Islington just to see her perform. Ah, those were the days!'

The account of the history of the little theatre caught Chiara's imagination totally. It was easy to see how enthralled she was and how reluctant she was to leave the library but Pina realised that they had taken up a great deal of time and started to make her move.

'If you're interested in other bits and pieces from the period,' said the librarian, 'I can give you the address of a friend of mine. He runs a second hand bookshop near Bloomsbury Square and specialises in theatrical ephemera.'

'Ephem…' asked Chiara. 'What was the word? And what does it mean?'

'Ephemera,' he repeated, 'and it means things left over from past times that were never meant to last but somehow escaped being destroyed. Like old photos, and programmes, and newspapers, and sometimes letters and cards. I know he has a great selection for example of those penny plain and tuppence coloured sheets of characters for toy theatres. You know about them, I suppose.'

Wide eyed in wonder, Chiara shook her head. But as she settled back into her chair to hear more, Pina realised again the time they had taken up.

'Perhaps that's for another day,' she gently suggested.

'Yes, yes…you must come and see me again said the archivist, realising what Pina was trying to do. 'I would enjoy that. And meantime…' and he took out a piece of paper and scribbled on it a name and address. 'Here's the address of the shop of my friend, Andrew. It's tucked away near Bloomsbury Square, not far from Sicilian Avenue if you know it. Quite old fashioned. Go and see him sometime and discover his treasure trove for yourselves.'

Pina and Chiara rose, shook hands and thanked their new friend over and over, promising to return soon.

Chiara's feet seemed hardly to touch the pavements as they returned home and at supper that night she regaled her father with all she had learnt.

Pina was astonished at how much Chiara had absorbed and when she had gone to bed and Pina was alone with Remo, they began to discuss an idea for the theme of Chiara's Christmas present.

'But let's see first,' said Pina, 'whether this is a nine day wonder or a lasting interest before we make too much of it.'

Ephemera

- One -

Although Chiara restrained her enthusiasm for a day or two, as the end of the week loomed she tentatively asked Pina how busy she would be on Saturday and whether there might be a chance of going to Bloomsbury.

Pina was delighted that the interest wasn't waning and they agreed on mid morning as a suitable time after the chores and before the need to prepare for Lola's and the girls' Saturday evening visit as it was their turn to come round for a meal and games of cards.

The number 38 bus took them right along Rosebery Avenue from the Town Hall and dropped them just past Sicilian Avenue from where it was but a short walk in the back streets to the Aladdin's cave of the bookshop.

It was tucked away at the end of its street and outside there was a stall with some old books at reduced prices which clearly were little more than jumble.

Pina pushed at the door and stood back to let Chiara enter first.

The shop was both dark and light. The height of the bookshelves made it impossible for light to penetrate fully all the time. The shafts that came through the big windows of the shop had to take their turn at illuminating the rows of books. To one side of the door was a desk, covered in papers and volumes and with a lamp, and the floor space all around was filled with mountains of brown cardboard boxes, each with a white label attached marked with spindly writing in black ink.

Behind the desk sat a middle aged man, so tidily dressed that he seemed out of place against his background.

As Pina and Chiara entered, he rose from his seat and extended a hand.

'Good morning, ladies,' he greeted. 'Are you just browsing or do you have a particular purpose with which I may be able to assist you this morning?'

Pina nudged Chiara…but she stayed silent.

'My daughter,' she began, again not without a little flicker of pride at the words, 'is looking for information from many years ago and we have been advised at our library that you're just the man who may be able to help out. I'll leave Chiara to explain.'

Now emboldened by the introduction, Chiara began.

'It's about the old theatre at the Angel.'

'Ah yes, now which one would that be? Do you mean Sadler's Wells?'

'No, the one that's now a cinema…the Islington Empire.'

'I know the one. How can I help? And how far back are you interested in?'

'The librarian said it was once a real theatre.'

'Indeed it was. And for a brief time, quite a famous one too. People came from all over London to see the shows, even Royalty at times. But that was way back. Nearly 100 years ago now.'

'That's the one I'd like to know about,' said Chiara. 'I don't know why. It's just so strange. We pass somewhere every day not really looking. Then suddenly we see it differently and want to know more.'

'I know exactly what you mean,' said the bookseller. 'By the way, my name is Andrew. It's good to meet someone so enthusiastic. And you are…Chiara, wasn't it?' And he held out his hand.

'Chiara…' he repeated. 'Hmm…almost a coincidence. One of the regular performers at the theatre in those days was called Clara which is an English version of your name, though it was really her sister who was the famous name of the day. They worked together there and worldwide. So, tell me what you'd like to know.'

'Do you have any papers or books about the theatre?' asked Pina, anxious to establish that they were there as customers not just to pick the bookseller's brains.

'Ah well,' Andrew replied, 'that may be a bit of a tall order. The answer is yes…somewhere…But, as you can see, my stock is not in the best of order. I buy a lot of things at auctions or from individual sellers but just don't have enough time to sort through it all and place it properly and organise it before another lot arrives, so I am always in a state of happy confusion. So it sits in boxes and in piles, on the shelves and in the basement. Oh yes, there's a downstairs as well. I have stock. But whether I can put my hands on it or not is a different matter. However, you're in luck with your request. Not long ago I bought a collection of programmes at auction. The previous owner or maybe the original owner had bound them together which means they have annoying holes in them but the thread is easily cut and I'll need to untie them and allocate them to their individual theatre boxes which I keep by name. In fact I've been working on some of them recently and know just how to lay my hands on them. I'm fairly sure I saw some programmes from The Grand or The Philly as it was called in the bundles I bought, though I don't have a specific box for that theatre as they are too few and far between to justify a box of their own. Give me a minute, will you, and…but perhaps you'd like to take a seat,' he said to Pina, offering her his chair, 'and the young lady can come with me, if that's alright with your mother?'

'Of course,' said Pina, accepting the chair as Andrew led the way to the back of the shop and waved his hand in the air to encourage Chiara to follow him.

Some ten minutes or so later the pair re-emerged with some boxes and large folders in bags.

'You see what I mean about my chaos?'Andrew said with a smile. 'But let's clear a space on the desk and work our way through. No, don't stand up, please,' he said to Pina who started to vacate his seat. 'I've a couple of stools here for us which will do for now. So let's see what we have here…'

He pulled out from the bags several bound bundles of paper.

'You can look too,' he said, offering a bundle each to Chiara and Pina, but they refused.

'Better for you to look as you know what you are looking for.'

'Fine,' said Andrew, 'but you can just look through as the programmes and bills are all from the period we are interested in. It will give you a feel for the time.'

And so with careful hands, all three turned over the pages of the bundles and saw theatre names and plays and operas and actors and a whole world of entertainment now buried in time flit across their gaze and once more come to light.

It was a while before Andrew turned a page and exclaimed.

'Oh yes, oh yes…and another and another here…' and he turned his bundle to where Pina and Chiara could easily see what was exciting him.

Some quite small pieces of paper, folded in half with close tight printing but on the top of each the title:

Royal

Philharmonic

Theatre

'There you are,' said Andrew. 'I knew there were some, and they're all together. So convenient and something of a miracle. If I'd started on these and unpicked them, who knows where they might have been scattered to by now!'

'The border round the printing is embossed,' said Pina, running her finger over the paper lightly. 'It's very pretty. A bit like lace.'

'And on the back page there's an advertisement for perfume,' said Chiara. 'What's toilet vinegar Pina?'

'…And look, the Princess of Wales uses this…Lime juice with glycerine for the hair after sea bathing…'

'Erm, ladies,' interrupted Andrew, 'there's a centre spread too, which may be of some interest.'

'Oh sorry, yes,' said Pina. 'Yes it's easy to get carried away. And I have no idea what toilet vinegar is. I suppose toilette would be better… but…never mind, let's just look and see. Open up, Chiara.'

'*La fille de Madame Angot*,' she read out. 'Well I know what *fille* means. It means daughter. We did it with Miss Roche and it's like the Italian *figlia*…but who is Madame Angot?'

'Look, it shows a lot of the scenes in a list and there's another play with it.'

'There usually were two or more things on the bill in those days,' said Andrew. 'The others were quite short. A bit like the B films and the News at the cinema now before the main film. But here's another. This one says that the theatre has been beautifully redecorated and improved.'

'*Giroflé-Girofla*. What a funny name for a play,' said Chiara smiling.

'Yes, that one's an operetta too by the same composer as for the *Fille*…a man called Lecocq. He was French. But these are translated into English.'

'Just look at this cover,' said Pina. 'It's got all the details of transport to and from Islington to all over London and it even says where to change and gives some fares as well. Just look at this…Conveyances to Victoria…painted green…until 11 pm…and those to Chelsea are painted blue and run till 11.30. And the fares…just look…2d and 3d.'

'But you paid 2d on the bus just now to get here,' said Chiara. 'And how long ago was this, Mr Andrew?'

'We're in luck,' said the bookseller, responding inwardly to the little politeness of the young girl in calling him Mr Andrew. 'The owner, the original owner of the programme who probably saw the shows has written a date in ink on the top. 1877. And here. But it says the show was first put on in Oct 1874. Sometimes the programmes actually have dates printed on them, but not always. What I don't seem to have is a programme for what was one of the most famous pieces put on there early in 1870s. *Genevieve de Brabant.*'

'I saw that name in the bundle you gave me,' said Pina. And she turned the pages. 'Ah yes, at the Gaiety theatre...Look, it says that it transferred here for Saturday matinee performances only. With the whole Philharmonic Company...led by...'

'Emily Soldene,' exclaimed Chiara with the pleasure of recognition.

'Yes indeed,' replied the bookseller. 'And I'm sure there's more here somewhere.'

'Perhaps,' said Chiara, 'we could help you sort out your papers. Or at least I could. I know Pina's very busy but I have lots of spare time.'

There was a quick flicker of a glance between Pina and Andrew as he replied.

'We would have to think about that because I don't make enough money here to be able to afford an assistant and...'

'Oh I wouldn't want to be paid,' said Chiara. 'It wouldn't be a job. I'm too young to be working like that. I was just thinking of helping you out...'

Pina remained silent, allowing Andrew to take the lead.

'Perhaps,' he said at last, 'perhaps your parents would let you come sometimes and give me a hand with some specific task. For example, when I decide to tackle these programmes and theatre boxes properly, which I can't face doing at present as I have too many books to deal with...' waving his hands round vacantly and hoping to be convincing.

'That sounds like an excellent idea,' said Pina at last, hoping to have struck a balance between practicality and not suppressing enthusiasm.

Chiara remained thoughtful.

'I suppose that does make sense. After all I do have to concentrate on the scholarship and my arithmetic is weak. But I really want to help.'

'And so you shall,' said Andrew. 'Let's leave it to your parents to work something out.'

'We should be going,' said Pina, looking at her watch. 'We have taken up the best part of Mr Andrew's morning. So now, Chiara, would you like to buy one of the programmes as a souvenir?'

'Oh no,' said Chiara, vehemently. 'They mustn't be split up. They've been together for so long it would be a shame.'

'But,' said Andrew, 'I'll have to split them eventually. No one will want to buy them all. So please take your pick and we'll cut the thread that ties them.'

'No, please,' said Chiara. 'Leave them together with their friends a while longer.'

'Alright then,' said Andrew. 'I'll leave the Gaiety bundle untouched until you come again. But this one…look! I can detach just one of the programmes, like so…' and he deftly took scissors from the desk and before Chiara could protest. Snip, snip. And *La fille de Madame Angot* was free from the bundle.

'Now,' said Pina, opening her purse…

'Now, nothing,' interjected Andrew. 'I have no idea what to charge anyway. I would need to work it all out by looking up to see what I gave for the whole collection etc etc…Far too much effort! And anyway I don't want to! I would like you to have it as a gift for your first visit and if you do come and help me out eventually perhaps that's how we might compensate you for your efforts.'

'I can't…' Chiara began.

'You can,' Pina interposed, 'because Mr Andrew is offering it as a gift and it would be hurtful to refuse.'

'Well then, if you're sure,' said Chiara picking up the folded sheet and placing it gently between the palms of her hands. 'Just think. This piece of paper was there on that very day when the opera was sung. What stories it could tell. What a life it's had. And now it's my treasure. Thank you, Mr Andrew.' And in a trice she replaced the programme on the desk with care, leant over and kissed him on the forehead, which took both him and Pina by surprise as had her little speech.

'Thank you, thank you,' repeated Pina getting to her feet while Andrew tucked the folded programme between a folded foolscap sheet of paper.

On the doorstep of the shop, Chiara said, 'Thank you so much for a wonderful morning.'

'And you too, my dears,' Andrew replied waving them off and smiling happily at the unusual way his morning had been spent.

Alice to the Rescue

The bus arrived at Bloomsbury Square quite quickly and as it pulled away from the stop and the conductress came along the aisle with her block of tickets and little 'cling'-ing clipper machine, Pina said to Chiara

'You get off at the Town Hall and I'll just pop up to Chapel Street for a couple of things. It might be a good idea for you to have a word with your father on your own. Oh yes, tuppenny and a penny, please. Thank you.' And the conductress clipped the two tickets and gave them to Chiara who divided them and handed one over to Pina.

'But I wanted you to be there when I asked Pappa about the bookshop. He always listens to you.'

'Perhaps,' replied Pina. 'But maybe it's time you learnt how to ask him directly for yourself. It'll give him the chance to make up his mind without being influenced by anything except what you say. Just be direct with him. But if you prefer not to say anything, leave it for the moment.'

'I'd rather you were there too,' said Chiara. 'But I'll see how busy he is when I get back. You won't be long will you? Do you need a hand with the shopping?'

'No, thanks, cara. Just one or two things for tea when Lola and the girls come later. Oh look, here's the Post Office already…get ready… ring the bell.'

When Pina arrived home about a half an hour later she found father and daughter sitting at the kitchen table. The kettle was already coming to the boil on the stove and Chiara jumped up and took the bags from Pina and made her sit down.

'Cup of tea?' Chiara asked.

'Oh, yes please. The market was heaving. Saturday afternoon, what did I expect? But I was in luck.' And here she dived into one of the shopping bags and pulled out a paper bag bulging with something clearly sticky.

'I took a chance this late in the day and popped into Restorick's on the way home. They still had these…' and she tore the paper off a sticky mass of buns, their tops all dark brown and glistening with the glaze.

'These are for us now, not for later,' said Pina, as Remo got up and went to get bread knife and butter dish.

'I was lucky,' she said, 'the last three…'

'And did you…?' asked Chiara hesitantly.

'Did I what?' teased Pina. 'Did I remember to ask for…' and she produced a smaller bag, '…these?' and handed it over to Chiara.

'What's that?' asked Remo, puzzled by the exchange.

'Oh, just crumbs,' said Chiara. 'Lovely, delicious, tasty bread crumbs.'

'Well actually they're the bits that come off the crust when they slice the bread for customers in the machine and they clear the trays frequently. I was in luck. End of the day crusty crumbs.'

'Mmm. Wonderful,' said Chiara coming and giving Pina a hug. 'Better than sweets, any day.' And she tipped the contents of the bag into a small dish, licked her finger and dipped it in. 'Mmm…lovely. Have some, go on…'

'No darling, you enjoy them,' said Pina. 'We'll save ourselves for the bun with our tea and then we'll have to get on with the pasta sauce for supper.'

'All under control,' said Remo. 'I started it while you were both out earlier. So, you can just sit down. We have something to discuss. Chiara's latest idea. I understand that you disapprove of her going to the bookshop, Pina.' He looked severe, very severe. Chiara was standing behind Pina as he spoke so Pina could not see her face.

'Oh, so she's told you…' she replied. 'But I didn't…'

And Remo's face broke into a smile.

'Sometimes it's so easy to wind you up! No of course she didn't say you disapproved. Nor do I, but there is a *but*.'

'Oh Pappa, there's always a *ma* in everything! Always a *but*! You know when we play the gramophone…on that record of Rosina's song… she sings a lot quite calmly and then pauses and suddenly says 'ma' and everything comes rushing out.'

'So, come on then,' said Pina, What's the *ma!* here?'

'The *ma!* here is a MA with capital letters,' said Remo. 'It's the Scholarship exam and what Chiara told me about being worried about her sums…arithmetic, sorry. That has to be her priority for the months ahead.'

'I agree,' said Pina, 'especially as she's seen that she's weak in that area herself.'

The tea was made and poured, the buns cut and buttered, rather lavishly, by Chiara herself and all three sat round the table as the conversation continued through drinking and sticky finger licking with Chiara occasionally dipping into the dish of crust crumbs.

'I think,' said Pina eventually, 'I'll try to get some old exam papers and we can do some practice at home. Or at least if we can see what the questions are like, we can make up some of our own.'

'Can you ask at the school? 'Asked Remo.

'Hmm, I doubt they'll give me anything there as it would be unfair to all the others. But I'll ask Fr Martyn if he can get me something from the Parish school. He knows all the teachers there and they must have some they can lend us. I'll have a word after Mass tomorrow.'

'And what about the bookshop?' asked Remo. 'You're keen to help out there, Chiara, aren't you?'

'Yes, really. I think it could be fun and helpful too.'

'Well I suggest that I come with you next week and we talk to your Mr Andrew together…about you going in the holidays when you can spend a whole day and really get something useful done. What do you think?'

'That's great,' said Chiara. 'Thank you, Pappa. And you too Pina, for taking me today and for crusty crumbs as well!'

When they were alone later, Pina turned to Remo.

'Do you think she's really worried about her sums?' She asked.

'Yes I do. But it's wonderful that she's telling us and not keeping it bottled up. You know Pina, this openness of hers with us has developed so well since you came into our lives. I'm so grateful to you.'

'Don't be silly,' said Pina with a smile. 'You did all the groundwork and it's paying off. But I do worry that the day will come when she grows out of it and starts wanting to keep things to herself. We all have that in our character,' she said looking at him with some significance.

But he dropped his gaze from hers.

'Let's hope that's not for a while yet,' he said, 'and when it does happen, I know you'll cope. You always do.'

And he put his arm round her waist and drew her to him with a hug and a long very affectionate cuddle.

'Yes,' she sighed to herself, 'not for a while yet. A long while, please God.'

- Two -

'Have you nearly finished those sums, Chiara,' asked Pina from across the kitchen, 'I'll be wanting to set the table soon for supper?'

'I'm on the last one now,' Chiara replied. 'Well it's not the last one really. I've done that already. It's the one I don't like doing because I always make mistakes so I leave it to the last.'

'Is it one of those divisions?' asked Pina. 'What do you call them, long divisions?'

'No,' replied Chiara, 'it's multiplication. I hate them. But only when they've got three numbers in them to multiply with. Why aren't they called *long multiplication*? They should be as they take so long to do.'

'Perhaps because multiplication is already a long enough word,' replied Pina, 'and it would make it even longer with a long on the front! I thought you hated division the most?'

'Oh, not anymore,' said Chiara brightly. 'You solved that for me ages ago.'

'I did?' asked Pina astonished. 'How did I do that?'

'Well, you and Alice actually,' smiled Chiara. 'You remember you were reading Alice to me one night. That bit where she's being told about school under the sea with the Mock Turtle. And they were talking about sums and I had to ask you what 'derision' meant?'

'Oh yes, and I had to look it up as I wasn't sure,' said Pina, 'and we found 'deride' means to mock or laugh at. But how…?'

'Well, once I knew that I could laugh at doing those sums, I felt better about them and soon got the better of them.'

The kitchen door opened and Remo came in to the middle of the conversation.

'Got the better of what?' he asked, joining in.

'Division sums,' said Chiara,' but Alice showed me how to deal with them,'

'But she's not happy with multiplication,' said Pina.

'So why can't Alice help you out again?' asked her father. 'What does she have to say about multiplication?'

'Nothing very helpful,' replied Chiara. 'The Mock Turtle calls it *uglification*.'

'What on earth does that mean?' asked Remo.

'Making ugly, I suppose,' said Pina.

'Well then,' said Remo, 'the solution is easy: your answer is *prettification*.'

'Ha ha,' said Chiara. 'There's no way you can make these long lines of numbers pretty. They just get more and more tricky especially with all the carried over numbers where there's no room for them in the boxes. I lose my way half way through the second line every time and it is all looks so…well…ugly!'

'Let's have a look then,' said Remo. 'Move over a bit. Can supper wait a while?' he asked Pina.

'Yes, no problem. It's minestrone, so it's ready when we are.'

'Let's see, then,' said Remo. 'You say you get into trouble with the second line, Chiara. So, let's do away with the three lines. It'll take a bit more writing out, but it will keep things clearer. Instead of one big sum, we'll make it three separate sums and then add up the answers at the end. Look, like this.'

And Remo wrote out the long number and underneath, neatly in the squares on the paper, he wrote the first line of the number to be used to multiply, simplifying it, and then he set out the second and the third sums in similar ways, like this:

$$\text{Sum to do: } 46{,}597 \times 472$$

$$
\begin{array}{ccc}
46{,}597 & 46{,}597 & 46{,}597 \\
\times\,400 & \times\,70 & \times\,2 \\
= \underline{18{,}638{,}800} & = \underline{3{,}261{,}790} & = \underline{93{,}194}
\end{array}
$$

$$
\begin{array}{r}
18{,}638{,}800 \\
+\ 3{,}261{,}790 \\
+\ \ \ \ \ 93{,}194 \\
\hline
= \underline{21{,}993{,}784}
\end{array}
$$

'You see,' Remo said, 'if you simplify it, you don't get confused with the numbers you are carrying and forget what you are doing.'

'Well, that's simplification,' said Chiara, 'not really prettification. But that's fine. And to be honest, it actually looks tidy, so I suppose it's pretty too! Can I try one now, please?'

'Just one,' said Pina, 'and then supper!'

Supper was simple – minestrone with bread, and cheese and fruit afterwards – and so took no time to serve once the table was cleared. When all the supper things were tidied away, Chiara asked if she could try some more, using Remo's method of setting things out and her parents were pleased to see how on each occasion, she achieved the correct result and more and more speedily too each time.

'Now that's enough for tonight,' her father said at last. 'I want to talk to you about something else. Could you fetch me the programme you were given when you went to the bookshop? I never really looked at it properly and I have had an idea.'

Puzzled, Chiara went to fetch it from her room and brought it to the kitchen table, folded inside its protective piece of paper.

'I was thinking,' said her father, 'that you could frame it.'

'But I can't,' said Chiara. 'If it goes into a frame, you won't be able to see all of it, part will always be covered.'

'Yes, I've thought about that,' said her father, 'but if we fold it out, like this,' and he took the delicate paper into his careful fingers, 'and make a double sided frame with glass on both sides, then it can be hung and turned around to see both front and back and not be damaged by being touched a lot. I just thought it might be better than leaving it in a piece of paper where you are too afraid to handle it.'

'Bravo, Remo,' said Pina. 'It's not too big so the glass won't be too heavy for a frame. What do you think, Chiara?'

'Could you do that?' Chiara asked, 'Or would you have to have it made?'

'I think I could manage it,' said Remo with a smile. 'In fact, I've already bought the glass... in case you were willing for me to have a go. Just choose what sort of frame you fancy.'

'How did you know the size?'

'Well, I have to confess…though you may be cross…'

'What's that?' asked Chiara, puzzled.

'I saw the folded paper lying about in your room on the table and took it out and measured it in case…I hope you're not…'

'Don't be silly,' said Chiara, getting up quickly to hug her father round the shoulders and kiss his forehead. 'Thank you, Pappa, thank you.'

'And while I was measuring,' Remo continued, 'I had a closer look. There's something I believe you haven't noticed. Look closely.'

And he spread out the programme before Pina and Chiara who studied it closely and then, shook their heads baffled.

'The name of the leading character,' said Remo. 'The daughter of Madame Angot.'

'Yes?' said Chiara still puzzled.

'Oh I see,' said Pina. 'It's a form of your name, Chiara, in French.'

'Oh yes,' exclaimed Chiara in surprise and delight. 'How silly not to have seen that before. La fille de Madame Angot is called Clairette!'

Sweet & Sour

-One-

Chiara tapped timidly at the Headmistress's door that confronted her. She did not know why she had been sent for this morning.

There was no reply.

She tapped again.

Again, no reply.

What should she do? Tap again or return to class?

Using her knuckles, she tried a third time.

The door was opened suddenly and filling the doorway was the form of her black-robed Headmistress, her face framed in its starched white surround over which hung the black veil. The suddenness of this apparition made Chiara start back and she was sure that she heard a sigh of exasperation as the sister exclaimed.

'Oh yes, Chiara Romani, yes, come in now.'

And as the nun turned towards her desk which was placed directly opposite the door that led into the room, Chiara saw the stiffness in her shoulders subside, so that by the time that the sister took her seat, her face was all wreathed in smiles and dimples, though behind her small, rimmed glasses, her eyes were as hard and unfeeling as ever and her smile was as artificial as any politician's.

'Yes, now, Chiara. One or two things. Firstly, it has come to my attention that your sums have improved a lot recently. So tell me, who is your new teacher who is helping you outside school?'

'Only my parents, Sister,' the child replied, standing before the desk and in the doorway.

'Close the door, dear,' said the nun, 'and come right in.'

But she didn't ask Chiara to sit down.

'Well, if you continue like this,' she said, 'you're bound to be given a Scholarship place.'

'I don't know,' replied Chiara. 'I would like to do my best for my parents.'

'And for your school, I hope,' Sister added swiftly. 'It's so important for us that you do well, you know. Have you talked about a new school at home?'

'Not really,' Chiara replied. 'I think I'll go where my cousins go.'

'Your cousins?' queried the nun. 'I didn't think you had cousins.'

'Well, they're sort of cousins through my stepmother,' Chiara replied openly. 'One has already passed and the other will do the exam when I do.'

'And where does your cousin who passed now go to school?' asked the nun.

'Our Lady of Sion was Franca's first choice and she got in. Rosa and I would like to go there too if we both pass.'

'Our Lady of Sion!!' exclaimed the nun. 'Holloway Road! Holloway!' she sniffed. 'I think we can do a bit better than that. Now there's a good school in Hammersmith and another in Finchley. We shall see.'

'But, Sister,' interrupted Chiara who was now getting a little agitated. 'I don't want…'

'What? You don't want…?' replied the nun severely, all trace of pink niceness bleached from her cheeks, 'Yes, well…well…' as she regained her composure… 'We shall see when the time is right.'

'Should I go back to class now, Sister?' asked Chiara.

'Erm, no. There is something else,' said the nun. 'Your father carves wood, doesn't he?'

'Yes,' replied Chiara, 'when he gets the chance.'

'Well,' said the nun, 'I would rather like a statue of an Angel to stand in the Hall, or the Salle. Perhaps he could come and talk to me about it?'

'I'll ask him, Sister,' said Chiara, 'but wooden statues are very expensive, which is why he doesn't get asked often.'

'Expensive?' queried the nun, 'Oh yes, well perhaps he might like to make an offering to your school. We shall see, we shall see. Well, back to class now, Chiara. Oh yes, by the way, do try to keep away from the gate that divides our school from St John's playground. You and other girls are spending too much of your play time down at that end of the playground.'

'Yes, I know,' replied Chiara, artlessly. 'Since Franca went to Grammar school, Rosa likes to come and see me every day at playtime and we chat together.'

'Yes, well,' replied the nun, shuffling papers on her desk and avoiding eye contact, 'you had better return to class now. Close the door after you.'

And Chiara obeyed.

When she returned to her class room, she sensed an air of disruption. She had missed reading poetry while she was with the Headmistress but she was in time for French and Miss Roche had already put up the familiar and much loved wall chart that showed the *French Farmyard of Yesteryear* with an array of clean and well behaved animals and birds hardly ever to be found gathered together in such an artistic way in reality.

Miss Roche was asking about the cats in the picture and Chiara slipped quietly into her seat without drawing attention to herself. She realised that Miss Roche was playing more distractedly than usual with the watch on her wrist, which she fastened there with elastic rather than a strap. When she fingered it a lot, it often sprang back and often made a snapping noise. Today it was doing overtime between her questions today about where the cats were sitting and what colour they were and if they had whiskers.

This always made the class laugh when they had to repeat *les moustaches du chat*.

Miss Roche poked wisps of hair into her bun and glanced repeatedly out of the window that looked out on to Duncan Terrace.

There was almost a sigh of the release of tension when a knock was heard on the classroom door and Sister appeared there accompanied by a very official looking man. The children of course automatically rose to their feet as Sister walked to the front of the room and with little more than a nod towards Miss Roche, announced.

'This is Mr Winterbourne. He has come to see your lessons today. Please make sure you make him welcome. I'll leave you in Miss Roche's capable hands,' she said, smiling pinkly and insincerely at the official and glancing coldly at Miss Roche, before beaming widely at the children and leaving the room.

There was an empty desk in the back row. Without a fuss Mr Winterbourne settled there and said, 'Hello children. Thank you for letting me spend some time with you today. Please pretend I'm not here. Do carry on with whatever I interrupted, Miss Roche.'

And the class settled without a problem back into the comparative merits of the whiskers of the cats and the tails of the dogs in the foreground of the picture.

Miss Roche was clearly back in her stride as her watch sat undisturbed on her wrist throughout the next twenty minutes before the hand bell clanged in the corridor to announce morning break. As the children were dismissed to the Salle for their milk and Ovaltine tablets, Miss Roche and Mr Winterbourne, both smiling, rolled up the farmyard picture and chatted in French animatedly.

The children speculated on who the visitor might be and came to no particular conclusions. He spent the next part of the day after morning break with them again as they practised their sums. He came round to look at their books and stopped at Chiara's desk, looking with interest at the way she set out her multiplication sums, and clearly impressed with their neatness and unfailing correctness, he said, 'Very good, Very neat. Keep it up.' And passed on to look elsewhere.

- Two -

The next day Chiara found herself once more outside the Headmistress' door. This time, she was holding the exercise book.

'Enter!' was the instant response to her knock and the nun made no move to shift from her seat at the desk as Chiara entered the room.

'Chiara Romani,' she began in an alarmingly hostile voice.

'I will not have rudeness to visitors in my school. I will not tolerate insolence. How dare you behave as you did yesterday? What do you have to say for yourself? Speak up!'

Chiara could feel the prickling of sudden tears at the back of her eyes. She was truly astonished at this attack. She remained silent. She always found that silence was a good way to deal with the unexpected. It cut the ground away from the attacker, gave them no hold, nothing to proceed with. And so it was now as in view of her silence and her lowered eyes, the nun had to recommence her onslaught.

'Show me that book. Open it at yesterday's work and show me what games you are playing.'

This was an order that Chiara could respond to and she turned the pages and laid the book, the right way round, on Sister's desk for her to see.

Neat rows of figures, each one tidily confined within the square allotted to it on the page and row on row of ticks in bright red ink.

The nun was clearly baffled.

'This is not how you have been taught to do sums, is it?'

'No, Sister… and yes, Sister,' replied Chiara at last beginning to understand why she was under attack.

'Explain yourself.'

'At school we learn one way; at home I was shown another.'

'You come to school to learn. That's what your parents expect of us. You are not here to follow your own path. The inspector made a comment yesterday which will not look good for the school report and you, little miss know-all, are the cause.'

'I'm sorry, Sister,' said Chiara meekly. 'I didn't realise I had done anything wrong.'

'In future you will do the work as you are taught here. Is that quite clear?'

'Yes, Sister, even if I get the answers wrong?'

'Tut. Don't be pert, girl! Get back to class and take this...' And she thrust the book across the desk at Chiara as if it were tainted somehow and would infect her pious hands if they stayed in contact with it any longer. 'Take this with you.'

'Yes, Sister,' and Chiara turned to the door and opened it a little.

She paused.

'Should I tell you another time what my pappa said about your statue?' she added, half turned to leave the room.

The anger and fluster suddenly drained from the nun's cheeks and her eyes sparked with a gleam of greedy interest.

She composed herself and said with an apparently disinterested sigh,

'Oh well you may as well tell me, as you are here now. Close the door for a moment.'

When Chiara faced the desk again, the harshness had been wiped from the nun's face and she was looking almost pleasant.

'My father says that it will depend on how large a statue you have in mind. He is happy to do the carving for no fee but the wood will be more expensive if you want a full size statue. He would want to use oak. So if you only wanted a small statue for the hall table to stand where St Anthony stands with the white stick, I'm sure it wouldn't cost that much at all.'

'Well, he could use something less expensive than oak,' said the nun, bridling a little now that it was clear that money would have to change hands.

'My father wouldn't do that,' said Chiara. 'He always says that if a job's worth doing, it's worth doing properly.'

'Yes, of course,' replied the nun. 'That's always the best way.'

'So should I not continue to do my sums the way that helps me get them right?' added Chiara.

'Oh enough now, child,' said the sister, irritated and dismissive. 'Talk it over with your teacher and do as she says. Now, back to class with you.'

'Thank you, sister,' said Chiara, making sure that no trace of a smile on her face could be seen as she turned to the door to let herself out.

At lunchtime that day when the children were allowed out from the Salle after their meal, Chiara found the gate that connected her playground with that of St John's, firmly locked.

Advent

- One -

The November sun was weak but bright as it illuminated the basement windows where the statue- painting took place. There was enough warmth in it through the glass for the girls not to need any heating. They were on their own. Just the three of them as often happened on a Saturday. Remo had gone off as usual for a wander round, shopping for supper which he always prepared on a Saturday, and a drink at the Italian club with his friends in Clerkenwell.

Pina and Lola had taken themselves off up West to mooch round the shops and try on clothes that they had no intention of buying and sample sprays of perfume and shades of lipstick that their budgets would never afford.

It was what they used to do as girls and it was always an enjoyable pastime with no expense involved beyond the bus fares and the visit to Lyons Tea shop, usually the one in New Oxford Street, where a coffee and a roll and butter would satisfy the need for a sit down and a chat before catching the bus home outside right to Finsbury Town Hall. They were relaxed as they knew the girls were trustworthy and could be left on their own without anxiety, and the three girls loved having the place to themselves for a few hours and were happy to set about the robes and cheeks and noses and eyes of the familiar range of saints, Sacred Hearts and Madonnas.

It wasn't often that Remo made a new mould and tried out a different pose for a Madonna or a saint. There was hardly any room for imagination with a Sacred Heart. The pose was set fast. But he varied the Madonna output quite regularly, apart from Our Lady of Lourdes which was as traditionally posed as a Sacred Heart. He had been working on a new saint lately but it was dubious whether it would catch on in popularity as she was not well known. Still it was worth a try and he made a few for his regular outlets to try out. He had explained to Chiara that he had wanted to make two figures, a male and a female: St Jude and St Rita. It was easy to create a figure recognisable as the latter in her nun's habit, holding a rose and with a thorn prominent in her forehead that characterised her story, but St Jude had been more of a challenge and so had been relegated to a future occasion when inspiration might strike. When Chiara had asked him what had attracted him to the two saints, he told her that a lot of people needed reassurance in their lives, so to have a saint who was especially in charge of 'hopeless cases' and another whose domain was 'the impossible' was a very attractive proposition. The conversation had arisen around the time of November 1 and 2 when All Saints and All Souls were celebrated, and both in school and in church there had been a concentration on what makes a saint.

This was the first batch of *Santa Ritas* and the girls were excited at being able to experiment with unfamiliar colour-mixing for the robes even though the face required traditional tints. By common consent, Chiara was appointed *paint-mistress of the thorn* as hers was by far the steadiest hand and there were no teardrops to exercise her talents at this particular time.

'Do you think they'll unlock the gate again soon?' asked Rosa who because of her name was appointed *paint-mistress of the rose* which was in the saint's hand. She had decided to vary the colour of the flower from statue to statue though her preference was for yellow.

'There's not a lot of difference between St Rita and St Theresa,' commented Franca. 'They're both nuns and they're both shown carrying flowers.'

'Yes,' replied Chiara, 'but their habits are different colours and St Theresa doesn't have a thorn in her forehead. I'm sure,' she continued, answering Rosa, 'that it's my fault that the gate's closed.'

'Why?' asked Rosa. 'Because we kept chattering there?'

'Yes,' said Chiara. 'Sister doesn't like it. She was really horrid about Our Lady of Sion as well'.

'But you *are* going to put it down as your first choice?' said Franca, 'Both of you, aren't you? It's really nice and so close.'

'Well,' said Rosa, 'I want to wait and see what Chiara does first.'

'So you might not come with me,' said her sister, very startled at this new thought.

'I think,' said Rosa, 'it's more important that we two stay together as we're the same age. You already have your own friends and go around with them a lot, but Chiara's my best friend.'

'And you're mine,' said Chiara putting her hand on Rosa's shoulder while waving her paintbrush in the air with the other. 'But let's wait and see what happens with the exams and what our parents say.'

'Well. Mamma says it's up to me,' said Rosa, 'and of course we don't know what Dad thinks. He writes every now and then and sends parcels but I sometimes think we'll never see him again.'

'Oh Rosa, don't say that!' said Franca, quite upset and with paint dripping onto her apron.

'Take care,' said Chiara, leaning over to steady Franca's hand, 'or you'll be painting yourself into a nun's habit!'

They all laughed and Rosa continued.

'Well, Mamma never talks about him and whenever I ask about him, she always brushes me off.'

'When does his service end?' asked Chiara, concentrating hard on the thorn in her statue's head to avoid looking directly at the girls in case she saw tears in their eyes.

'He's in the Forces, permanently,' said Franca. 'He has to go wherever the U.S Government sends him. He hasn't been over here for years, as you know, and I'm not sure that Mamma wants him back either the way she behaves when he's mentioned.'

'Did they meet during the War?' asked Chiara.

'Yes,' Franca replied, 'and they married quite quickly. But apart from the wedding photos and one or two of them holding me as a baby at the christening there aren't many pictures of him. He never sends any.'

'I've only seen him twice that I can remember,' said Rosa, 'when he was here on leave for a while. There are some snaps from then with us all in them. I think we went to the seaside somewhere on a train.'

'Yes,' said Franca. 'We got the train at Victoria and went to Broadstairs. We both had ice creams from an Italian shop on the cliff top and made sandcastles and went in the sea. It was a lovely day. But Mamma hardly ever talks about Dad so it's quite odd. It's as though he doesn't really exist.'

'I don't like to upset Mamma by talking about him,' said Rosa. 'But that's not to say I don't think about him a lot. You're so lucky, Chiara, to have a Dad and a Mamma too.'

'Don't forget,' said Franca hastily butting in, 'Chiara had no Mamma for years until Zia Pina came back from Italy.'

'I never knew my real mother,' said Chiara, 'and my Pappa never talks about her at all so I am a bit like you two.'

'Perhaps that's why we get on so well,' said Franca thoughtfully.

The conversation was light and just punctuated the concentration on the painting until the front door was heard opening upstairs and Remo's voice in greeting boomed down at them that a cup of tea would be very welcome for someone who had just done heavy shopping for supper.

The girls hastily laid aside their brushes and made for the kitchen upstairs to answer his request and satisfy their own need for a break.

- Two -

Saturday supper. When Remo prepared it, it was always the same: sausages. Italian sausages, well sausage rather than sausages as it was bought in one long coil and then chopped up at home into smaller pieces. It was a little on the spicy side, so Remo always made mashed potato and varied the greens according to the season. Chiara's favourite was spinach but she knew that this took a lot of cleaning and boiled down to almost nothing so for six people, a huge amount was needed and she never requested it, but her father knew her preference and often bought it none the less and prepared it all himself when he was in charge of the meal. Such was supper on this Saturday and Remo saw Chiara's eyes light up when she caught sight of the bags of spinach on the kitchen floor.

The speciality of sausage Saturdays which at most were every two weeks was the pot of *mostarda di Cremona* which Lola and Pina loved. This delicacy, if that is the right word for something that seemed to burn into your taste buds, was bought in quantity at Christmas time every year and eked out over the twelve months. It came in sealed tins which Pina decanted into glass jars with tight fitting seals as it was important for the air to be kept out of the fruit or the special strength evaporated.

The girls loved the bright jewel-like colours of the crystallised fruits that gleamed through the golden sugar syrup but no one could identify how the fruit was given that kick of heat that made it so different and exciting. The most potent of the fruits were the cherries, perhaps because they were small and so were infused with the syrup most thoroughly but the most attractive were the tiny mandarin oranges sliced in half as the colours of skin and flesh just shone in golden splendour. Clearly there was mustard involved in the processing but not the sort of mustard you could easily buy in a grocer's shop.

This Saturday's supper was significant. Only a few fragments of fruit lay in the syrup at the bottom of the jar and there were no more tins in the cupboard. The stocks had run out just before the new Christmas season started, just as should happen, although Pina had been prudent enough to reserve enough pieces of the fruit and some syrup to meet the demands of the recipe for the *tortelli dolci* without which no Christmas would be complete.

The four weeks of Advent would see no sausage and *mostarda* suppers and after Christmas, things would start up again as usual.

Having breaks from treats is a valuable lesson to be learnt.

This last supper of the season was a good one as of course there was a lot of syrup to use up even if the fruit was sparse.

It was while Lola and Pina were ooh-ing and aah-ing over these last dregs of *mostarda* with their girls laughing at how excited they could get at something so silly that Remo suddenly stood up at the table.

'I have decided…' he said, and there was something about his gesture and his tone that took them all by surprise. A sudden ominous silence descended. A fog infiltrated the clarity of their chatter.

'I have to leave.'

The lightness of the atmosphere totally evaporated and the girls sat, stock still and silent.

Then he turned, abruptly, and left the room.

All eyes turned on Pina who shrugged her shoulders and lifted her hands in a gesture of complete bafflement.

A few seconds passed that seemed much longer, perhaps a minute or two but the audience remained still.

The door reopened to reveal Remo holding a piece of paper in his hand.

'I'll be off on Monday,' he said, 'to get my ticket for the boat train at the end of the month.' And he laid the paper on the table before the assembled company.

The top portion of the sheet showed an embossed crest.

The papal crown and keys.

Pina picked it up and scanned it quickly and then looking round at the others said, 'This is a summons from the Vatican Museum in Rome. They're asking Remo to put in a tender for restoration work on some medieval wood carvings. He has to attend for an interview on Wednesday next.'

'I only knew about it today,' Remo said seriously. 'The letter was waiting for me care of the Italian club. It's been there a while. I have to go. I cannot pass up this chance. If I get the work, it'll mean being away again for a while next year but there will be several other applicants, better qualified than I am so it may come to nothing. All expenses paid for this trip anyway but the connections are not good and I'll have to break the journey overnight in Paris on the way back.'

The addition of the details went some way towards lessening the shock of the news.

'Oh, you had us all scared,' said Chiara reprovingly. 'You are funny Pappa!'

'That's what I'll be saying if the Pope makes a joke at supper,' replied Remo with a smile as he tousled his daughter's hair. 'Sorry for being so dramatic. It has been worrying me all day, what I should do. And it was the *mostarda* that convinced me. Don't ask!'

The atmosphere had been somewhat restored by this exchange and Pina helped it on its way.

She looked at the clock.

'If we don't get a move on,' she said, 'we'll miss the start of Variety on the radio and there's a good line up tonight.'

'Get a move on with what?' asked Lola, surprised.

'Well, the Christmas outing at least,' said Pina. 'We have to decide if we want to go this year or else we won't get decent tickets.'

'You're right,' replied Lola.

'So, girls, what will it be this year?' asked Pina.

'Could we give Tinkerbell a miss for a change?' asked Franca meekly.

'Oh oh oh' chorused Rosa and Chiara together. 'We love Peter Pan. Oh please.'

'Well, Franca has a point.' said Pina. 'We've been for the last three years at least.'

'Oh it's not Christmas without Peter Pan,' said Rosa.

'Let's just see what else there might be.' said Lola.

'I've seen posters,' said Remo, 'for something called *Rainbow's End*.'

'That's been on for years,' said Lola. 'We might even have seen it as girls, Pina.'

'I think you're right. Is it the one with the flying carpet?' asked Pina.

'Flying carpet?' said Rosa, suddenly enthralled.

'Yes,' replied Lola, 'and St George, I think, but I don't recall much else.'

'Oh if there's a saint in it we'd better go,' said Chiara laughing. 'It might be good for business and give Pappa some new ideas!'

And they all laughed, the air of gloom having passed from their midst as swiftly as it had descended.

'What's it called again?' asked Chiara.

'Not *Rainbow's End*,' said Lola, 'but…'

'*Where the Rainbow Ends…*' Pina added. 'That's it. *Where the Rainbow Ends*.'

Christmas

'Pappa, do you think I'm old enough yet?'

The family was sitting round the table on the first Saturday morning in December. Chiara's question took Remo by surprise.

'That depends,' he replied cagily. He had been caught out before now by his daughter's forthright approach.

'If you want ear rings, then *no* is the answer and will be for ages to come. If you want to go shopping in the West End on your own, then *no* is the answer as I don't want you in those crowds of Christmas shoppers. If you want to spend the day painting all the statues I'm behind with, then of course you're old enough.'

Chiara laughed. 'No, none of those things...yet!' she said. 'Though I am happy to paint some statues later if Pina doesn't need me for anything.'

'Just help with the bags in the market,' said Pina. 'But that won't take long this morning. So come on then, what is it you have in mind?'

'Well I was wondering if we could go to Midnight Mass this year.'

Remo glanced across at Pina.

'How do you feel about that, Pina? Will it make preparing lunch too much of a rush if we don't get to bed until quite late?'

'It will be different, certainly,' said Pina. 'But most of the preparation is done in advance anyway. Hmm. You've given me an idea, Chiara. What if we have our main meal on Christmas Eve and then go out to Midnight Mass later? Christmas Day would be mainly cold things and take less preparation. We could sleep in if we wanted. After all the family isn't coming round this year until Boxing Day so it would be just the three of us to please ourselves when we do anything. But it wouldn't be the same as usual. Breaking tradition...how do you feel about that, Chiara?'

Of course when Chiara had asked her question she'd had little idea of the ramifications so she took her time before answering.

'It sounds exciting,' she said at last. 'If you're sure that it's not going to disturb things too much.'

'Not at all,' said Pina.

'Well then,' said Remo, 'I suggest we go somewhere a little further afield for Mass. Just a little longer walk. No, don't ask. It'll be a surprise. We may have to leave about 11. So maybe we'll all need a doze after our meal as it will be a long evening.'

'Thank you both,' said Chiara, getting up from the table. 'I'll go and get ready for us to go shopping, Pina. 'The sooner we're back, the sooner I can help Pappa with the painting.'

When Chiara had left the room, Remo turned to Pina.

'I have a question for you,' he said. 'Do you think Chiara's old enough?'

Pina smiled. 'For what?' she asked.

'For us to let her go to the bookshop on her own on the bus. She hasn't asked but I was thinking that she'll be going a few times during the holidays and it might be good for her to learn how to fend for herself a bit. After all, next year she'll have to do the journey to school on her own. She won't want us taking her and picking her up. I just thought we could get her used to journeys on her own. What do you think?'

'You read my mind,' said Pina. 'The thought often flashes into my head but I forget to raise it with you. It would be a good idea to make the offer before she asks. Let's see how she reacts. But I don't want her going to school on her own yet. While she's at the Convent, it will be business as usual, if you don't mind.'

'I agree,' said Remo. 'The pattern is secure and I see no reason to change it.'

'I'll be taking her to the bookshop next Saturday,' said Pina. 'I'll broach the subject then and she what her reaction is. Maybe I'll suggest she comes home on her own. But at a particular time.'

'Well that's going to solve one problem,' said Remo.

'What's that?'

'We shall have to get her a watch for her Christmas present. Well, one of them at least. I'm already dealing with her main one.'

'Yes,' said Pina. 'Very mysterious…a locked room! Hmm and no hint to me about what's going on there!'

Remo tapped his nose and smiled. 'My secret,' he said.

- Two -

As they approached the bus stop outside the Town Hall on the following Saturday, Pina broached the subject.

'Chiara,' she began, deliberately imitating Chiara's pensive approach to topics. 'I was wondering. Do you think that you are old enough?'

Chiara was intrigued. 'Old enough for what, Pina?'

'Old enough to do this journey to the bookshop on your own?'

Chiara was clearly taken aback. It was not something that had crossed her mind at all and the suggestion caught her off guard. Her reaction was to put her hand onto Pina's arm.

'Not now?' she asked. 'You don't mean now, do you? I don't think…'

'No, not today, cara. But we just thought that maybe during the holidays if you go to the bookshop, you might like to try the journey on your own. Think about it. Don't worry about it though. I am more than happy to come and pick you up and take you at any time as you know. Oh, here's the 38 now and it looks quite full. We may have to go on top. Let's hope there's no one smoking.'

There was room inside however, at the front, and as soon as they settled, the conductress came along with her wooden block of tickets and the clipping machine.

'You ask,' said Pina, giving Chiara a shilling, deliberately avoiding giving her the right money.

'Tuppenny and a penny please,' said Chiara confidently, and after she received the clipped tickets, she counted out the right change she was given to return to Pina.

The journey passed in silence as they both looked out the windows at the little bits of Christmas decoration that the shopkeepers had strung up to make their windows festive. As they approached Sicilian Avenue, Chiara automatically got up and pulled on the bell cord, not knowing if the stop was compulsory or request.

As they approached the bookshop, she clutched at Pina's arm.

'You will come for me. Won't you?'

'Of course, cara. At about 3.30, as usual, depending on the traffic. I'm sure Mr Andrew won't mind if I'm a bit late. And knowing you, you'll have something to finish off before you're ready to leave. Here we are now.'

As they reached the shop doorway, Mr Andrew waved a welcome and opened up. Pina waved but didn't stop to chat, just to see Chiara safely indoors, and then she left.

When she returned that afternoon, she passed a little time chatting to Mr. Andrew while Chiara put on her coat and scarf. On the steps of the shop, Chiara took Pina by surprise.

'Can we pretend, Pina?'

'Pretend what?' asked Pina, puzzled.

'Pretend that you and I aren't travelling together on the bus. Let's sit separately and pay our own fares. Is that alright?'

'Of course, cara,' Pina replied beaming. 'I don't mind really if you're ashamed to be seen out with me. No really, I don't mind at all.'

'Don't be silly,' said Chiara. 'You know it's not that at all.' And she squeezed Pina's arm and could easily see that Pina was teasing.

'Just one thing, though,' said Pina, 'you'll need this.' And she pulled out a few coins from her pocket and put them into Chiara's hand. 'I suppose you'll be needing a purse now. Oh well, Christmas is coming. Who knows what you might find in your stocking from Father Christmas this year!'

- Three -

The pattern of days was undisturbed in the weeks that led up to Christmas. Chiara gained confidence in travelling with but separately from Pina to her bookshop duties. On the last visit before the holiday they took a small parcel of Italian treats as a present for Mr.Andrew. Pina had made an extra large batch of *tortelli dolci*, an Italian version of mince pies, with a filling of roasted chestnuts, glacé cherries, mostarda and alcohol in a sweet crumbly pastry case. They looked like fig rolls but there the resemblance stopped. As Pina wished Mr. Andrew a merry Christmas, she added, 'Oh yes, my husband would love you to come to dinner with us in the New Year. Perhaps one Saturday after work Chiara could bring you back with her. Remo is really keen that you should come. He says that you'll know why.'

'I shall be more than delighted, and we'll fix a date when Chiara comes back after Christmas to help out during the holidays.'

'Have a happy Christmas, Mr. Andrew,' said Chiara, 'and thank you for looking after me so well. It's such fun working in the shop.'

'And really helpful for me too,' replied Mr. Andrew.

'I am now getting on with so much that I have been neglecting since you started and it's good to have company. This is a little something for you. But no peeping until Christmas day. I'm sending it to your father to keep under lock and key until the day.'

And with a broad smile he handed over to Pina a flat wrapped parcel. They shook hands and Chiara spontaneously gave him a warm hug before they took their leave and he waved them off down the street.

- Four -

The weeks of Advent always seem to take forever to pass and this year was no exception. The anticipation of Christmas was heightened by the knowledge that this year the pattern of days was to be different. Eventually Christmas Eve arrived. There was a flurry of last minute food shopping but all the major preparations had been made. As usual Remo had commandeered the kitchen on the previous day, had banished the ladies and had set to, making the ravioli. He did this just twice a year at Christmas and Easter. He made the pasta and painstakingly rolled it out thinly and packed in the stuffing and ran the little roller round the parcels; hundreds of small packages; enough to last for a few days and to feed visitors. He also made the stuffing for the capon that would be boiled for the *brodo*. This was the major treat of the holiday as the stuffing cooked while the chicken boiled in the pot, absorbed the rich flavours of the soup and leached its own richness of parmesan cheese, onion and herbs into the liquid. It was best eaten cold and sliced and as it was so popular, Remo always made a second portion wrapped in muslin and cooked in the soup pot. It took time and when Remo cooked he liked to be left alone. The contribution that the ladies made was to the washing up after he had finished. So the festive meal was always a joint effort and enjoyed all the more as a result.

This year of course the main meal was on Christmas Eve and was finished by about 7 o'clock. The family enjoyed the ravioli in *brodo* and the chicken with its *pien* as their stuffing was called in the northern dialect. They had decided that pudding would be on Christmas Day in the English tradition though Pina started the long steaming process while the kitchen was already full of steam and cooking heat. So for dessert they had some of the *tortelli dolci* as they settled by the fire to listen to the radio. They all dozed a little but were awake by 10 p.m.

'If we leave by 10.40, we'll have plenty of time,' said Remo, still maintaining silence about their destination for Midnight Mass.

They muffled up against the cold evening air and set off in the direction of Exmouth Street market. Remo deliberately led them through back streets to disguise the route but Chiara was not to be fooled.

'It's the Italian church in Clerkenwell Road,' she said. 'It's an Italian Christmas isn't it, Pappa?'

Remo tapped his nose and shrugged as if to say that his secret had been discovered and as they crossed into Clerkenwell road he deliberately made his way towards the steps of St Peter's church. Just as they prepared to climb the steps however, he crossed the road and diverted towards Hatton garden.

Pina had guessed by now where they were heading, but for Chiara it was still a puzzle. Eventually Remo led them into the main road that runs down from Gamages to Smithfield and they arrived in front of an enclosed dead end. There was no sign of a church; just a gatehouse and railings.

'This is Ely Place,' said Remo, 'and the oldest Catholic church in London.'

And sure enough just inside the railings and to the right was the shape of the church with its narrow entry porch and steps down to the crypt.

'This is St Etheldreda's,' said Remo. 'We're in good time for carols.'

Chiara was intrigued as they made their way along a short cloistered passageway. To her right was an entry to the crypt but they passed it by, climbed a few ancient steps with a slight turn, and entered the main body of the upper church. A screen masked the main seating area from the entrance and gave a feeling of privacy and seclusion. There were no electric lights on, only candles everywhere, lighting up the old beams and columns. It was clear that behind the altar was a great stained glass window but without light from outside it was impossible to make out the design. Many of the pews were already full, but they found good seats half way along and it wasn't too long to wait before the lone voice of a chorister from outside could be heard with the opening verse of a familiar carol. He was joined by the choir, and the entire congregation rose to welcome them as they filed in for the carol singing that prefaced the Mass.

Gradually the main lights were raised and soon the effect of the flickering candles against ancient stone was absorbed into the greater light.

'*Lumen de lumine*' thundered the choir during the Creed and Chiara was swept along by the mellifluous repetition of the Latin plain-chant.

When Mass ended, Remo led Chiara and Pina down the steps into the crypt which was lit only by candles, so the magic atmosphere that had set the evening off was restored. Here they visited the crib scene with the baby lying amid fresh straw in the manger.

'Have you ever made crib figures, Pappa?' asked Chiara as she looked at the faces of the shepherds. 'I think you could make faces that are much more alive than these. And you could add other figures to make the scene more real, like the innkeeper and his wife and some other animals…'

'Don't get carried away, Chiara,' said her father. 'Tradition is very strong when it comes to crib scenes and churches can't afford a whole Bethlehem of people round the manger.'

'But in Italy,' added Pina, 'some churches do have whole scenes full of people, just on a smaller scale.'

'Yes,' said Remo, 'we shall have to make sure that we go and see these great traditions one day. And who knows, I may get a commission.'

Chiara closed her eyes at the crib and made a secret wish.

- Five -

When they emerged from church they didn't go through the gates they had used before. Chiara was startled as her father took a sharp turn to the right and led them into a dark narrow alleyway.

'Follow me,' he said, and with some excitement at the hidden route, Chiara and Pina followed him into the gloom, only to emerge suddenly into Hatton Garden.

'Wasn't that a pub we passed?' asked Chiara. 'What a strange place to have one tucked away. It probably gets very little light. It's so secret. Can we come again in daylight?'

'Of course,' said Remo, 'but there's another secret to show you before we return home. Don't worry, Pina,' he said, catching her look of anxiety about the hour of the morning. 'It's on the way.'

And they walked briskly along Hatton Garden, towards Clerkenwell Road, crossed in front of St Peter's, which was clearly still very occupied with Midnight Mass, and strolled down Saffron Hill towards the pub The Coach and Horses, where in the middle of the road Remo came to a sudden stop.

'Quiet now,' he commanded, and Chiara and Pina just stood with him in the middle of a deserted road in total silence. There was no traffic at that time of night so all was still. Then he beckoned them to a grating set in the road.

'Look!' he said. 'And listen!'

And they heard the noise of rushing waters beneath their feet. As they peered in darkness into the grill, they could see the movement of the water.

'What is it?' whispered Chiara.

'Just sewers?' asked Pina. 'But there's no smell.'

'No,' replied Remo. 'We're standing on top of the river Fleet, a hidden river of London that rushes on beneath our feet every day of our lives, unseen, unappreciated, unloved, unknown.'

'Where does it start?' asked Chiara, mesmerised.

'In Highgate and Hampstead,' Remo replied, 'and you can walk its course over ground all the way to the River Thames where it pours out. A lost River. It pleases me to think that we live on the banks of a river even if we cannot see it now. It makes me think of Italy and my old home there in the hills. But come on, it's late and bed time waits. It's not long until dawn now and we should all be asleep sooner rather than later.'

And so almost reluctantly they withdrew from the sound of the Fleet and returned home where the fire they had left banked up still glowed with warm coals to welcome them and the hot water bottles that Pina had left in their beds gave them a cosy end to a lovely evening and encouraged their eyelids to close very speedily in welcoming sleep.

They awoke later than usual and Chiara was aware that her parents were not stirring when she arose. So she made her way to the kitchen and boiled a kettle, hoping that she would get to make her treat of a cup of tea in bed before either of them stirred. Even if they did hear her clattering about, Pina and Remo had the sense to stay in their room and wait for the door to open.

'Are you still sleeping?' asked Chiara as she pushed open the door. 'Come on now, lazy bones, it's Christmas day. Maybe this will wake you up.' And she handed her sleepy parents their cups of tea.

'Happy Christmas, cara,' said Pina, 'and thank you.'

'What no biscuit?' asked Remo, teasing.

'Well, actually…' said Chiara. And she slipped out of the room again for a moment and returned with the plate she had left just outside the door with her own coronation mug of tea.

'I hope you like them, Pappa,' she said. 'Pina helped me make them and we hid them to surprise you.'

'Come in, cara, and snuggle in with us,' said Pina.

And so she did and the three sat sipping tea together.

'Perfect start to a perfect day,' said Remo. 'Well at least I hope it will be.'

It was Remo who made the first move to get up.

'Stay there, both of you,' he said, 'until I call you and then we'll have breakfast.'

And he was gone in a trice.

- Six -

He was away for some time which caused both Pina and Chiara some puzzlement, but eventually through the open door of the bedroom they heard a totally unfamiliar sound. Two voices wafted up the stairs in song.

Pina and Chiara looked at each other, astonished. It was clearly the gramophone and a very old recording in French of two very accomplished singers. When it ended, Remo called up.

'You can come down now,' and as they hurried to put on their dressing gowns, the music was played again and they heard the opening words: *Jours fortunés de notre enfance* – 'happy days of our childhood'.

The gramophone was set up in the sitting room and as they entered, they found the fire blazing nicely and on a table to one side, something quite large, covered in a cloth.

'Sit there, Chiara, please,' her father suggested, pointing to a chair in front of the table. 'And if you could help me, Pina, by taking two corners of the cloth and lifting it with me on the count of three, after I have reset the record.'

He lifted the arm of the player, turned the handle a few times to wind up the machine, placed a record on the turntable and, once the turntable was rotating, he lowered the needle into its groove. The familiar hissy scratchy sound at the start of the record started up and Remo signed to Pina to stand on the other side of the table.

'One…two…three…' and the cloth was carefully raised, to the wide-eyed amazement of Chiara.

There before her eyes stood a model theatre, beautifully constructed and painted.

'But it's…it's…our theatre…up the road…' she gasped, 'How did you? How did you?' And she was up out of her chair to go to her father but he raised a finger and she sat down again obediently.

Pina joined her as her father first reset the record on the player to the original side and then raised the curtain of the theatre to reveal a little painted set with cardboard characters in full costume.

'Do you recognise the scene?' he asked.

'Of course,' Chiara replied. 'It's Clairette visiting Madame Lange. But the scenery, the figures…I don't understand. How did you…?'

'Let's have breakfast and I'll explain everything. Oh yes, but first you have to open your present from your friend, Mr Andrew.'

And Remo passed Chiara the parcel which had been kept carefully out of sight until today.

She unwrapped it carefully. It was clearly a small book.

'Oh!' she gasped. 'I've not seen this before.' And in her hands lay the Book of Words as the Victorians called them for *La fille de Madame Angot*, all in the English translation that was used for the production at The Philly.

Chiara beamed at her parents and there were tears in her eyes.

'Come on now,' said Remo. 'Porridge is on the stove. Cold morning so warm breakfast.'

And Pina smiled to see such happiness between father and child as they left the sitting room, arm around shoulder and headed to the kitchen.

Over breakfast all was revealed.

How Remo had visited Mr Andrew and the Library and had made sketches of the proscenium of the theatre to assist him to build the frontage as accurately as possible. The backstage construction was conventional but he had visited Pollock's theatre shop for some ideas. Mr Andrew had found him a programme from a later production which had vignettes of the characters in costume and he had carefully redrawn these to scale and painted the little flats appropriately. But the triumph had been finding the records and these came from one of his trips to France where he had sought them out in old record shops there.

All of this he had achieved secretly and as he worked behind closed doors, not even Pina had had an inkling of what he was planning.

Later in the day, she would come to reflect on this quite seriously.

After breakfast there were other gifts to exchange and unwrap but nothing could keep Chiara from returning to her theatre and discovering all the other scenes and characters that her father had made for her.

Jours fortunés de notre enfance

Such was the theme of this Christmastide.

Rainbow's End

- One -

'I bet you're sorry you're not coming with us today, Pappa,' said Chiara over breakfast. 'I'm sure you'd enjoy it.'

'Perhaps, cara,' Remo replied as he dipped a piece of fresh bread dripping with butter into his bowl of milky coffee. 'But perhaps not...' as the morsel of deliciousness disappeared into his eager mouth, leaving a trail of butter on his beard.

In the pause that came as he savoured the treat, Chiara waited, patient and silent. Before Remo dipped another piece of bread, he said, 'I have seen the interior of the theatre before and as I don't know anything about this play you're going to see I really think I should try and catch up with some of the orders I've neglected lately.'

'Oh, of course. I'm sorry. I didn't think. You've spent a lot of time on my present lately and it must have put you behind. I just wanted you to share the day with us.'

'Well, as I said, cara, I have seen the theatre and it's amazing inside. I took your mother to see some opera there a while back, or dance or something. You'll love the inside.'

'You took Mamma? But how so? I thought she never came to England.'

'Sorry, cara, I meant Pina. I forget sometimes. Sorry if I upset you.'

'Not at all, don't be silly,' replied Chiara. 'Pina is the only Mamma I know.'

'But you don't call her mamma,' said Remo.

'Well that's because I got to know her first as Pina and that always sounds more comfortable. But I sometimes call her mamma.'

'And I know she likes it when you do,' replied Remo.

'Yes we went to the Stoll a couple of times. I have to warn you though, and I'm totally serious about this: don't get any ideas once you see the stage.'

'Ideas? About what?'

'I'm NOT making you a version of that stage. It would take me all my time from here to next Christmas and beyond. And now, may I finish my bread and coffee before it gets cold?'

'Of course. I won't bring home any commissions. Well, not major ones any way. Maybe…well…who knows? But Zia Lola says there's a fight between St George and a dragon so I might get you to…'

'Grr. Off with you, little pest,' said Remo with a smile. 'Go and help Pina with something and let me get on with earning the crust I'm allowed to dunk in my coffee when there's no one to nag me. Oh yes, I have a commission for you today. I expect you to take in every detail and tell me the story at bed time. It'll make a change for you to tell me a story instead of the other way round.'

'Sounds good to me,' replied Chiara. 'I'll go. But before I do, can I just ask you something?'

'What now, cara?'

'Does it upset you to talk about Mamma? My real Mamma, I mean.'

'Not at all,' replied Remo looking directly at his daughter. 'I just keep my memories to myself as they are not part of our lives together now. But I'm happy to talk about your mother whenever you want.'

'Yes I do sometimes want to know something or other about her,' said Chiara, 'but it's never anything important. I never knew her, so I don't really miss her. Not like I would miss Pina if something ever happened to her. Or you even. Well, I think I'd miss you…but who knows?' And she got up from her chair lightly, kissed the top of his head, ruffled his hair and disappeared before he could reply.

- Two -

The journey to the Stoll was the usual route that Chiara and Pina took to the bookshop. Lola and the girls had called for them at home first and they all went off together. The journey was less familiar to Franca and Rosa so when the bus reached the top of Southampton Row and Kingsway they were surprised at the tunnel that opened up in the middle of the road.

'Is that where the trams used to go?' asked Rosa.

'Yes,' replied Pina. 'But they stopped them a while back. How long, Lola? Do you remember?'

'I remember the last one going down,' said Lola. 'We came to see it off from work. Not that long ago, maybe a couple of years. I used to like the trams.'

'Especially this bit of the route where you go down here and come out right by the River,' added Pina. 'I miss them.'

'Why were they stopped?' asked Chiara. 'I think we went on them sometimes but it's a while ago now. I just remember going down here to the River when we went to the Festival.'

'Who knows?' said Lola. 'They make these changes, always supposedly for the better, but it rarely happens that it is. And who knows what use they'll make of these underground tunnels now: useless spaces after so much work to create them in the first place. Car parks probably or something more hush-hush for wartime.'

The conversation ended as they alighted to walk down to the massive frontage of the Stoll theatre where the banners proudly proclaimed *Where the Rainbow Ends*.

The three girls were overwhelmed by the extent of the theatre and even more impressed once they entered the auditorium and found their seats. It was vast and elaborate.

'No wonder Pappa didn't want me to get ideas about him making me a copy of this stage,' Chiara said to Pina.

'He did a great job with the Islington Grand,' said Lola. 'It's amazing how much detail he included. By the way, girls,' she added to Franca and Rosa, 'don't forget to thank Zio Remo for the tickets today, will you. Remember, this is his Christmas present to us.'

The girls nodded while examining the programme to see what sort of characters and scenes there might be to come.

Excitedly Rosa noticed a lion cub and a genie, while Franca drew her finger under the scene description '*where lost loved ones are found*' and looked at her sister.

As the curtain rose, the audience settled and the light overture gently set the scene: an extraordinary library rather poorly lit, but for reasons that would become obvious later on.

Chiara's thoughts were on the opening of Peter Pan and the much more cheerful Night Nursery of the Darling children but whereas it was clear that those siblings were loved and cared for by their parents, the brother and sister in this household were far from happy under the jurisdiction of their uncle and aunt. The atmosphere was gloomy and Chiara was aware of a sinking feeling from Franca on one side of her and the beginning of restlessness from Rosa on the other. But Rosa's interest suddenly bounced when the lion cub made its entrance as a sort of Nana substitute and Chiara's own attention sparked at the mention of a magic flying carpet. Though the plot was supposed to occupy the audience, Chiara's interest became sideways focused on the practicalities of the carpet and how it might fly and whether it would carry people on it. She could see no obvious equipment to enable the flying such as was immediately visible when Peter Pan and the Darlings flew.

Her heart sank when the Genie made his appearance through the carpet from below and yet she still hoped.

But the effects were going to be minimal and her keen eyes spotted how the grey cloak that masked St George on his entry was whisked off into the wings. So when all four children with lion cub and the Genie stood on the carpet and wished it away, she wasn't surprised that the lights faltered totally and extinguished for a few seconds, even though through the back window moments later, the carpet with silhouette figures could be seen outlined against the moon.

The consensus in the first interval was that the story was alright so far but not especially exciting even though the flight of the carpet had been superseded by the appearance through the smoking trap door of the dragon king.

'*Hmm*,' mused Chiara. '*That's a shame. There probably won't be a good fight for St George later on if it's only a dragon king and not a dragon*.' But she kept her thoughts to herself.

There was enough of interest in what followed to divert all three youngsters, especially Rosa, as the lion cub took a major part in the proceedings and the staging was really old fashioned in a lavish picture book sort of way. But when the last act started and journey's end was in sight, Chiara felt Franca stiffening beside her. She put out her hand and Franca grasped it. Of course the ending was happy. There were beams and smiles all round by the final tableau as the ship with St George at the prow began its voyage home from where the Rainbow ends with children and parents reunited and a rosy future ahead.

The hustle and bustle of the audience leaving the theatre excitedly talking about this scene and that, which had fired imaginations, distracted Pina and Lola from noticing anything odd about Franca. As Rosa insisted on walking between the two sisters, arms linked in theirs, Chiara found herself walking back with Franca. She was aware of her cousin's silence.

'You don't have to tell me if you don't want to,' she said at last. 'But if you can, just say why you are unhappy.'

Franca sighed.

'It brought it all back,' she sighed. 'Everything I've been thinking about over Christmas. My dad. Lost to us. Don't know if he's even alive.

Not even a card this year. Mamma doesn't say anything, just carries on, but sometimes I see her crying. So Rainbow's End where lost loved ones are found was just a bit hard to take today. No magic carpet and St George for me. I don't think Rosa takes it so badly and I don't want her to know what I feel. Oh Chiara. I'm so sorry. You may be just as upset as I am. I didn't think.'

'No I'm fine, Franca,' said Chiara, reassuringly. 'There's a big difference. My mamma is dead and I never knew her. So there is no chance of ever seeing her. But with your dad, well, there's always hope and the thought that he can be found again one day. Just try not to let it upset you too much especially as there's nothing we can do about it and we can't call up St George. Look at it this way: at least we don't have horrible uncles and aunts looking after us. We are really lucky with the people we have. Well I am anyway. If I didn't have Pina, I wouldn't have you and Rosa and with you two I don't feel so alone.'

Franca smiled. 'Thank you, Chiara. You're good for me too.' And without more said, the two girls linked arms and caught up with the others by the time that they reached the bus stop.

- Three -

Later that evening when supper was over and all the dishes cleared away, Remo turned to Chiara.

'Right! Time for bed!' he decreed.

Chiara looked puzzled and checked the time on her new watch. 'But it's very early. I thought there'd be at least another half an hour.'

'You've forgotten your promise already then,' replied her father glumly.

'My promise?' said Chiara, 'Oh no, not at all. Of course, I said I would tell you about the play at bedtime.'

'And I presume that will take some time,' said Remo. 'Well I hope it will. I'm expecting the full version. Unless it was so boring that it will take only a few minutes.'

'No,' replied Chiara. 'I've lots to tell you and something serious to ask you as well.'

'You'd better go and have your wash then and get ready for bed,' said Pina. 'I have already put the bottle in the bed and the fire's on so you won't be chilly. Your father will be up in a while. So as you wash your face, you can get your thoughts together. I'll be up when you have told your tale just to say goodnight.'

By the time Chiara was ready for bed, Remo had already made himself comfortable in the painted wicker chair in her room. It creaked under his weight as he shifted about.

Chiara soon snuggled down.

'Now,' she began, and she faithfully related all she could from the opening swish of the curtains. 'Do you want me to tell you what I thought as I go through the story?' she asked, 'or leave that to the end?'

'Story first please,' said Remo, 'thoughts later.'

'Well…' And so Chiara continued, describing scenes but only what happened not what she thought about events and people.'

When she finished, Remo gently clapped his hands.

'Brava, cara,' he said. I enjoyed that a lot. Not sorry I wasn't there though. It all sounds a bit sentimental and old fashioned to me.'

'That's why it's nice,' said Chiara. 'It's different from how we live now. If I have one thing to say about it that I thought was strange, it was the boat at the end. Where did it come from? And how was it going to get them all home again even with St George leading the way? And who rowed it?'

'Chiara, you have to – what we say about stories – suspend your disbelief.'

'What does that mean?'

'You find something impossible to believe because it's not logical or doesn't make sense, but you just pretend that it does so as not to spoil the enjoyment of the story as a whole. It only works with stories, not with real life.'

'So to enjoy the play, I should forget about the ship's sudden appearance? Is that what you mean?'

'Well, yes. Look. If you can accept a genie coming out of a carpet, it should not be too difficult to imagine how a ship appeared.'

'And what about a place where lost loved ones are found? Should I believe in that too?'

'Well we think of heaven as that place, don't we, cara,' said Remo gently.

'Yes, but that's for people when they die,' said Chiara. 'Do you think there's somewhere for people who aren't dead but just lost?'

'Not an actual place where they are gathered together,' said Remo. 'No. But wherever a 'lost' person is, is that place where they can be found or from where they can escape. You know Chiara, it was much easier when you came back the first time from seeing Peter Pan and wanted me to write and ask for a little fairy dust so that you could fly. Much easier. Why this seriousness? You look sad.'

'Not for me, for Franca. She misses her dad so much. He's lost to her and she doesn't know how to try to find him.'

'Well, I'll promise you this then, Chiara. But you must give me your word not to talk about it to anyone, not even Pina. Your solemn word.'

'I promise. Not a word.'

'I shall do what I can to track him down. I may get nowhere but I'll do my best. I'll tell you what I do every step of the way, but you must say nothing, not even a hint. Because if I fail, we would have raised false hopes for Lola and the girls and their sadness would be worse in the long run.'

'I understand,' said Chiara leaping out of the bed to give her father a hug. 'Should I call you St George from now on?'

'Cheeky!' smiled her father, kissing her forehead. 'But now, sleep. Or Pina will be telling me off. Not a word now, not even to her.'

'Night, night. Pappa. And thank you, for everything.'

'Sleep tight, cara and God bless.'

The Letter

- One -

The sun was streaming into the windows of the upper floor of the house in Duncan Terrace where the top two years of the Convent School were taught. Lessons were continuing as usual on this bright morning but the children were aware that Miss Roche was a little distracted. The wisps of her hair that were usually so neatly tucked into her bun had somehow developed a freedom of their own and were misbehaving and she was plucking at the elastic strap of her watch more frequently than usual as her pupils worked away at their sums. Suddenly the cause for her distraction became clear as the doorway of the room was filled with a dark shadow that did not pass and in response to a tap of the ruler on the teacher's desk, the class all dutifully rose and stood by their desks as the formidable presence of Sister Angela manifested itself.

She was clearly in a good mood as she was smiling with her mouth at least if not with those sharp eyes that hid behind the tiny glasses on her nose. 'Sit down, children. Thank you, Miss Roche.' And she waved her hand at the teacher as if to indicate that she too might sit.

'I have here,' she continued, revealing from beneath the front folds of her habit her hand which held a bundle of small brown envelopes, 'letters for your dear parents, which I want you to deliver without fail when you go home today. They are very important and so I want you to collect them from Miss Roche at the end of the day in case you lose them. I shall need your parents' replies over the next few days so please remind them as often as possible. I think that they will all be pleased with what they are about to read and so will you. So let us stand now and say a prayer of thanks for all the good things that are showered upon us. Gratitude should always be shown and expressed.'

The children arose as the hands of their head teacher joined in prayer and her eyes closed. They waited to be led into some familiar phrases, but none came. Nothing but silence. They watched as Sister's eyes remained closed and her lips slowly moved. Then as her eyes started open, theirs dutifully and just as suddenly shut and remained so until they heard an 'Amen'. With a quick turn, she was gone, leaving the pile of envelopes held by a rubber band on the desk. The children sat down again and after some shifting in their seats and puzzled looks at each other, continued their sums as if nothing had happened.

Miss Roche undid the band and shuffled through the envelopes, checking each one off against a child in the room. Satisfied that their names and faces matched, she replaced the band.

Several hands were raised simultaneously. At random, Miss Roche pointed a finger.

'Can you tell us what those letters are about, please?'

Miss Roche sighed and then smiled.

'Yes, my dears, they're your scholarship results and there's nothing to worry about because this year everyone in the class has passed. Well done, all of you. You've brought great honour to your school and pleasure to me as your teacher.'

At the end of the afternoon, the children were all handed their envelopes and told to put them away carefully. Chiara tucked hers into her coat pocket and patted it as she made her way down the narrow stairs and out of the front door. It was the day when there was Benediction at St John's Church and so the whole school was always led in silence from one location to the other. Parents could come as well and they sat in the main body of the Church, but the top class always had the privilege of going into the organ loft. This was a mixed blessing as it was a cramped space and the stairway walls shed white powder dust on coats as children went up and down. But watching the service from up above was much better than being on the flat. The traditional hymns began against the loud wheezing and rumbling of the organ. By the time it was concluded and the children were released – some relishing, some rebelling against the upward drift of the incense – most thoughts of letters had gone out of their heads. Certainly when Chiara came out into the sunshine and saw not her father as she expected but both Pina and her sister Lola waiting for her, nothing was further from her mind.

She skipped down the steps to give them both a hug. 'What a lovely surprise,' she exclaimed. 'Are we meeting Rosa too?'

'Of course!' replied Pina. 'Your father had to go off suddenly this afternoon. He had a letter that needed some attention so I met Lola for lunch and told him I'd pick you up. Let's walk round and meet Rosa.'

'And then,' said Lola, 'I'll treat us all to tea and a bun at the Blue Kettle.'

Chiara felt the letter in her pocket when she heard mention of her father's letter and was just about to take it out and give it to Pina in case she forgot it when the thought struck her: *'What if Rosa didn't pass? What if she hasn't had a letter today. Or it was bad news?'* She didn't like the idea of that at all and she withdrew her hand from her pocket hastily.

Rosa came running out of the gate clearly delighted to see Chiara with her mother and aunt. But there was no mention of any big news, so as they all walked off together in the direction of the Blue Kettle all thoughts of school were lost in the usual exchanges of conversation about what they had listened to on the radio since last they met and what they might be doing at the weekend.

- Two -

When Pina and Chiara eventually reached home, Remo was already back and was busy with the evening meal preparation. Chiara rushed in to greet him and he put one finger on the side of his nose and tapped it and then moved his finger to his lips and looked serious. Chiara took the hint not to ask more as Pina was bustling about and eventually they were all settled around the table for their supper.

Remo asked about Chiara's day at school, at which point she remembered the letter.

'Sister gave us a letter to bring home,' she said. 'I'll fetch it.'

'After your supper,' said Pina. 'It's bound to be a bill and it can wait.'

Knowing the contents of the letter and wanting it to come as a nice surprise for them both, Chiara contained herself and finished her meal.

As she got up and made her way into the hall where her coat was hanging, there was a sudden surprise knock on the front door.

She stood back and called out, 'Pappa!'

'Coming, Chiara,' said her father. 'That's odd at this time of night.' And he unlocked the front door. 'Oh, hello Harry,' he said, and he looked puzzled as he came face to face with his next door neighbour on the doorstep.

'Everything alright?'

'Oh yes, no problem, Mr R.,' said Harry. 'Sorry to call so late but the missus forgot until just now. This came for you this afternoon. But there was no one in, so they knocked on us.' And in his hands he offered the parcel which he had put by his feet while he had knocked.

'Sorry if I startled you,' he said.

'No problem, Harry,' said Remo with a smile. 'Thanks for taking it in. Strange time for a delivery though.'

'Even stranger, really,' said Harry. 'They just left it on the step, hidden, and knocked, and by the time Pauline had opened the door, they were gone.'

'Well, please thank her for taking it in for me,' said Remo.

'Actually,' said Harry, 'it's not for you but for your little girl.'

'Oh?'

'Yes, and from abroad as well,' added Harry, curiously. 'Well the stamps are foreign. Italian I think.'

By now Chiara had emerged from behind the front door and was standing in the doorway next to her father.

'As it's for you, Chiara, you'd better take it.' And he handed it over into Chiara's arms.

'Thank you Mr H.,' said Chiara, 'and please thank Mrs H. for me too.'

'No trouble at all, my dear. See you around, Remo,' said Harry as he turned to go.

Chiara had thrust her letter into the pocket of her dress as she put out her arms to take the parcel.

'Pina, Pina,' she called, as she made her way back to the kitchen. 'Look what's arrived.' And she placed the brown paper parcel firmly on the table for all to see and wonder at.

No one spoke.

Whenever Chiara received a present, there was always a bit of a performance. She liked to savour presents. So she would feel and squeeze a parcel, try to get some idea of what was inside, let her imagination run riot and then make a silent guess. This extended the business of giving and receiving gifts at Christmas and Birthday times into quite a ritual as she enjoyed it when her parents played the same game with their presents. Pina and Remo now devised ways of disguising whatever they had to give and boxes of different shapes were used whenever possible to conceal the true nature of the gift within. So it was with this new arrival. Dishes were already cleared away after the meal so there was space.

'Hmm,' pondered Chiara, looking at the parcel. 'It's bulky but quite light. Look at the stamps, Pappa. They're not the current issue at all. These are quite old but the postmark isn't clear enough to read. And there's no return address for the sender. This is very curious.'

Remo made no comment but kept an enigmatic smile on his lips while Pina suddenly felt a shaft of cold air on her shoulders, shivered and was disturbed without knowing why.

She did notice, however, that the brown paper did not look that old and worn. There was something odd about having old stamps on newish paper. But she said nothing.

'I can't feel anything at all,' said Chiara, gently squeezing at the sides of the parcel, 'so I think it must be just a box but the cardboard is thin.'

'Let's snip off the string,' suggested Pina, offering the kitchen scissors which she had taken from the drawer in the table.

Carefully, so as not to waste the string, Chiara cut at a knot and then started to unfold the paper.

There was some thick tape at the joints but again she took care to ensure that the paper was intact and eventually, on the table stood a plain brown cardboard box with a lid.

She folded the paper and twirled the string tidily while looking at the box and after a pause, she lifted the lid and peered inside. On the top was a long envelope and this was resting on a number of smallish items, each wrapped individually in tissue paper.

Chiara moved the envelope and took out one of the small tissued packages.

'It feels like a little animal,' she said. 'It has legs, and a head with a funny shape…oh…that's a trunk, I'm sure. You feel, Pina.'

'Could be,' said Pina, handing the item to Remo who also felt it carefully.

'Yes,' he added. 'A trunk and large ears. Just unwrap it, Chiara and take a look.'

So with care, she unfolded the edges of the tissue to reveal a small grey elephant made of felt with pinkish lining in its ears, and toes marked out with small white patches. Its eyes were also tiny pieces of overlaid felt, stitched with great care. Its trunk curved into a sort of question mark and it looked when flat as though the head might make the figure topple over but no, once it had been restored and plumped up from lying flat in the packaging, the little figure stood squarely on its four legs and the trunk trumpeted into the air.

'It's delightful,' said Pina. 'Just look at the work that's gone into those stitches.'

Remo took it into his hands and rubbed his nose against the trunk.

'Not quite as big as mine,' he joked, setting the elephant down on the table.

'There are lots more,' said Chiara looking into the box. 'Where are they from?'

'Well, perhaps the letter may hold the answer to that,' said Remo. 'Perhaps as it was on top, you should read that first.'

Chiara took the cream envelope into her hands and using the scissors as a paper knife, neatly slit it open.

There was one sheet of paper inside. The writing was in sepia ink and very small and thin. There was no address or date at the top. It began, '*Caro tesorino mio*,' and was all in Italian.

Chiara scanned it and then looked at Pina.

'Could you read it for me please and tell me what it says. I don't know if my Italian is good enough to work it all out.'

'Of course, cara,' said Pina, taking into hands that trembled just a little.

With a glance at Remo who almost imperceptibly nodded, Pina began, '*My dear, darling little treasure…*' Pina faltered.

Chiara looked up at her father.

'So this is from you, Pappa?'

Remo shook his head.

'So it's from…'

'Yes, cara, from your mother. That certainly looks like her handwriting. She must have written it before you were born when she was expecting you.'

'Please, Pina, tell us what she says,' asked Chiara urgently.

- Three -

The short pause had given Pina a chance to run her eye down the page and a further shaft of cold had struck her.

'*Everybody needs an ark*,' she continued. '*You never know in life when storms will strike and you have to have somewhere to hide in safety. I cannot give you much but I promise that I shall try and make as many little friends for you that I can. The sisters have to help me sometimes as my fingers aren't always as nimble as they once were. I can't make an ark out of felt as it would just flap about but I'm sure your uncle will make you one out of wood if you ask nicely. He's a good man. So I'm not making a figure of Noah for you. He'll be your Noah, I'm sure. Lots of kisses, your devoted mother.*'

Pina handed the letter back to Chiara in silence. She took it, refolded it and replaced it in the envelope. 'Thank you, Pina,' she said. 'And now, how do we start?'

And without more hesitation, she started to unpack the tissue parcels from the box.

'Do you mind if we all join in?' she asked. 'I mean, if I divide the parcels into three piles and we all take a turn at guessing what they might be. If we're correct we get to keep the figure and we'll count up at the end and see who has the most.'

'Good idea,' said Pina, 'so come and sit down, Remo.' And she cleared the wrapping paper and string off the chair.

The guessing game was absorbing and new rules were introduced as it progressed, like giving ownership of the pair of animals if you guessed right or having to yield yours if you were wrong.

It lasted a long time. Pina and Remo both seemed eager for it to be leisurely and when at last it ended, an array of beautifully crafted felt animals stood proudly on the kitchen table in pairs.

'I think there's one left in the box,' said Remo.

Chiara peered in. 'Oh yes, just one! You have it,' she said.

'No let's all guess,' he replied, taking it from Chiara and tapping it slightly. 'Standing animal, four legs. So may be a horse.'

'We have horses already,' said Pina taking it from him, 'and there's something on the head. So maybe it's a deer.' And she handed it on to Chiara who felt round the head carefully.

'Aha!' Chiara exclaimed. 'That's why there's only one in the ark. I think it's…' And she carefully unfolded the tissue paper to reveal a pure white figure. 'A unicorn!' As indeed it was.

'Pappa?' she said.

'Yes, cara. It's late and you should have been in bed before now.'

'I know,' she replied, 'but can I ask you something first?'

'Of course, cara.'

'The letter said I have an uncle. Do you know him?'

'I did,' said Remo, looking at her steadily. 'A long time ago.'

'So is he dead?' asked Chiara.

'He's gone,' said Remo, 'so I suppose I'll have to make that ark for you or I'll have no peace. Now bed, young lady. You have school tomorrow.'

'Oh! School!' cried Chiara suddenly. 'I forgot in all the excitement. Sister gave us all letters today. I was just getting it when there was the knock on the door. Here it is. I'll go up and get ready for bed.'

'And we'll be up later,' said Pina as Chiara disappeared from the room taking with her the little unicorn.

Pina replaced the figures in the box as Remo slit open the envelope.

He read the contents silently and then with a big smile handed the letter to Pina.

'It's a new beginning,' he said. 'Thank you, Pina, for all you've done to make this possible. I could never have done it alone.'

'Ready!' a voice called from upstairs.

'Let's go up together,' said Remo, 'and congratulate our girl.'

And putting his arm round Pina's shoulders, he guided her out of the kitchen.

'...EVER AFTER.'

Daughters

- One -

'We'll have to look sharp this morning, Chiara,' said Remo at the breakfast table as Pina deftly managed to slide a piece of toast onto Chiara's plate already buttered and honeyed, while finishing her own cup of tea.

As it was a Saturday morning, Chiara had taken her time about getting ready so she was a little startled by her father's business-like address.

'We're going on a little expedition,' he explained.

'But Mr Andrew is expecting me at the bookshop,' said Chiara, 'and I can't...'

'Don't worry about that,' said Pina, 'I went to see him yesterday and explained you wouldn't be going in today.'

'But why?' asked Chiara.

'You'll see,' said Pina with a smile. 'Eat up your toast now. There's time for another piece. And have your milk. We're not that pushed for time.'

'That's right,' said Remo, 'but we have to be at Angel tube by 9 o'clock. That's when I asked Lola to be there with Rosa.'

'Rosa?' said Chiara. 'Only Rosa, not Franca?'

'Eat up now and you'll see in due course,' replied her father, getting up and clearing away his plate and cutlery.

Because both her parents were busy, Chiara munched quickly at her toast and drank down her milk faster than usual, then moved speedily to clean her teeth and get her coat on. She was back in the kitchen and ready before Pina and Remo had finished tidying the breakfast things away. She sat down primly, folded her arms and smiled.

They both laughed.

'Come on then,' said Remo, and he and Pina took down their coats, checked that the gas was out and that they had keys, and all three left the house with a spring in their steps in the direction of Rosebery Avenue, taking the little passageway down the side of Alice Owens School in the direction of the tube station on City Road where they saw Lola and Rosa waiting.

'Have a lovely morning, darlings,' said Lola after greeting Pina and Remo.

'We won't be late in bringing her back,' said Pina.

Rosa and Chiara just looked at each other, puzzled and shrugged their shoulders in bafflement as Remo went to the ticket office and they heard him asking for two adults and two children to Edgware.

The end of the Northern Line: Edgware. Much of the journey had been in the open air, so it felt as if they were travelling into the countryside rather than just to an outskirt of London. The girls spent the time looking out at unfamiliar landscapes. A trip on the Underground was in itself unusual for them as they generally took a bus to where they needed to go, and rather surprisingly their area of exploration was quite circumscribed. So to be out and about was an adventure. When they arrived, Chiara noticed Pina looking long and hard at the station clock and at her watch and then comparing notes with Remo.

'This way, girls,' he said. 'Well, I hope it's this way.' And he led them out of the station, turning left along a neat parade of shops. Within a few minutes they were on a busy main road. They crossed over and were surprised to find themselves at quite a narrow entrance to what looked like an avenue. After the hustle of the main road, there was sudden tranquility.

It was a different world.

Trees crowded along both sides of the road. Their leaves were still young but by the summer, they would shade the walk. They hid the houses that were set back behind lovely front gardens and a grass verge ran alongside the pavement. But the surprise came almost at once as on their left appeared a pond from which scurrying across the main road came two geese and a duck. As the road twisted slightly to the left, the whole length of the avenue now stretched before them. The houses were beautiful but the trees forming the guard of honour on either side of the road were magnificent. Nobody spoke as they just walked on and on, slightly upwards towards a destination that stubbornly refused to reveal itself.

An apparently dead end when viewed from a way off turned into a narrow lane and on one side a great expanse of park opened out while on the other stood two unpretentious gates, open.

The girls looked at each other bemused as Remo ushered them in smiling. There to their left was an amazing cedar tree. It was this that caught their eyes first and then as they turned to see what faced it, they were stunned by the grace of a grand old mansion, not quite a palace but more than a house.

'Where are we, Zio?' asked Rosa.

'At what may be your new school,' Remo replied.

Chiara looked at Pina, her face full of bafflement.

'Just take a look around,' said Remo, 'and see how you both feel.'

They looked up at the front of the old house.

'Look!' said Chiara. 'There are little faces in the corners of the windows!'

'Where?' asked Rosa. 'Oh yes, I see them, right in the corner. Are they angels?'

'Cherubs, I think,' said Remo.

There did not seem to be any problem about wandering around and they could see the extent of the park that fronted the house even though it was fenced off. Around one corner of the building, through an ornamental arch, there was a large paved area, in old stones, a sort of terrace that had steps leading down into parkland as spacious and gracious as the one at the front. At the bottom of some steps, a path led to the start of a long avenue of lime trees, and just round from there, to their delight, was a large pond. Everywhere there was bird song filling the air.

They explored in silent wonder. Remo and Pina said nothing, but exchanged many significant looks as they noted the girls' reactions.

As they left by the same narrow gate, Chiara began, 'We're not sure what you meant, Pappa...about our new school.'

'Well, cara, we thought you might both like to go to school together as you grow up, and somewhere a bit nicer than where we live.'

'But we thought we'd be going to Our Lady of Sion,' said Chiara. 'Like Franca. She loves it there.'

'Yes,' said Rosa, 'but she's made her own friends now and has less to do with me. I'd rather be with you.'

'That's what we thought,' added Pina. 'Your mother and I have discussed it and she's happy about your going to a different school from Franca.'

'But, Pappa,' said Chiara, 'this looks a bit grand. Will it be expensive to come here?'

'With a bit of luck, no,' Remo replied.

'Just the fares and your lunches,' said Pina.

'But there's a catch,' said Remo.

'Which is?' asked Chiara.

'You'll both have to sit an entrance exam and then have an interview. You have to pass both and then the local authority may agree to pay the fees and so it will cost very little. As Pina says, fares and food. But you'd have that anyway.'

'It really depends,' said Pina, 'on whether you both like the idea enough to go through another exam.'

Chiara and Rosa looked at each other and each nodded seriously.

'But what if…' Chiara began.

'Bridges can't be crossed until you reach them,' interrupted Remo. 'Now we'll find a cafe and have a drink and then back home. Lola is making lunch for us.'

'So, have you decided then?' asked Pina.

'Yes, Zia,' Rosa replied. 'I think there's no doubt. It's worth a try. Thank you, Zio Remo.' And she grasped his arm tightly as they were walking along and hugged it as Chiara did the same on the other side.

- Two -

On Monday morning it was Remo who took Chiara to school.

There were one or two other parents lingering outside the front door of the school after the children had gone in.

Eventually one of the nuns emerged.

'Sister will see you now,' she said. 'Please come in. This is a busy time for us so please be patient. If you wish to make a more precise appointment, I can do that for you. Otherwise you may all have to wait quite a while as Sister talks to you all.'

Several of the mothers looked at their watches and then approached the nun with requests for other times which she wrote in a notebook, asking them to make a note for themselves. The small group dwindled considerably and Remo knew he wouldn't have long to wait. He and a couple of mothers whom he knew to wave to sat in a line along the wall, like grown up children waiting to be called in to see the Head. They realised the amusing side of this situation and chatted amiably. Remo was happy to let them go in before him and he had brought a paper to read. He waited about forty minutes before the door of the office opened a nun invited him in.

'Sister will see you now, Mr Romani,' she said, stepping aside to let him in and closing the door after him.

Sister Angela did not rise from her chair to greet him and her eyes behind her severe little glasses were if anything more brittle than ever. Her lips managed a smile and she waved her hand at a chair.

'Good morning, Mr Romani. Thank you for dealing with this so promptly. It should not take long.'

And she deftly slid a sheet of official paper from one pile on her desk in front of her and took up her pen.

'I take it we are dealing with Chiara's secondary application.' And without waiting for an answer she began to write.

'Yes, Sister,' replied Remo.

'So, name, date of birth, scholarship details,' she reeled off as she wrote out the lines of information.

'First choice...Our Lady of Sion. Second choice...Now do you have a preference?'

'Errrm, first choice, Sister, is not Our Lady of Sion.'

'Oh!' she said sharply, 'Oh? So you intend to send Chiara to Hammersmith?' She sighed. 'To the Sacred Heart. Well at least...'

'Actually, Sister, no,' interjected Remo. 'We wish to put down as our first and only choice, North London Collegiate School for Girls.'

The nun's body clearly froze in her seat. Eventually she raised her eyes to settle steadfastly on Remo. The glare was that of Medusa and held him transfixed. Only her lips moved.

'That is not acceptable,' she said at last. 'It is not a Catholic School.'

Perhaps it was because she was looking at Remo through glasses that the effect of petrifaction did not take place.

'But that is our wish, Sister, and I would like you to write that on the form for me,' Remo replied calmly and steadily.

'But our authority does not send girls to that school,' the nun continued. 'I believe it is out of our area for secondary school transfers. They will not allow you. Unless of course you wish to pay fees.'

'If that is necessary, then I shall do that,' said Remo. 'But I have set my sights on that school for Chiara, if, of course, she is capable of passing the examination and the interview.'

The podgy fingers of the nun's left hand flattened over the sheet of paper which she had been filling in. Slowly they contracted into a fist, pulling the paper with them and tightening it into a ball; she removed her hand from the desk and deposited the screwed up form into the waste paper basket by her chair. Then, smoothing the paper before her, she began a clean form.

'North London Collegiate School for Girls,' she said as she wrote in the appropriate space.

'Thank you, Sister,' said Remo with a warm if insincere smile, more of humour than of gratitude.

- Three -

It was on a school day, about a week later that Pina was faced with an envelope in Remo's hands when she returned from taking Chiara to school and from a little shopping in Chapel Street. He placed it on the table and made two cups of coffee with hot milk. They both sat and looked at the envelope. He pushed it with one finger towards her. She turned it to face her, hoping to see that it was addressed to just Remo but, no such luck; it was addressed to Mr and Mrs.

She picked it up, sighed and opened the flap. She took out two sheets of paper folded together and putting them on the table pushed them with one finger in Remo's direction. He unfolded them, read them, without betraying any indication on his face of their contents, refolded them and passed them across to Pina. She seized them, unfolded them and read the news and a great smile spread over her face and was reflected on Remo's.

'So what next?' she asked. 'What do we do now?'

'This is only the first stage,' Remo replied. 'Just dates and times for the examination and the interview. We must keep an unexcited attitude about it all in case it comes to nothing. I don't want Chiara to be made anxious.'

'I expect that Lola will have had a similar letter from the school. You could check with her when you collect Chiara later, if you would.'

'No problem,' said Remo. 'I just hope their interviews are on the same day, so that they can go together. Well, Pina, this is the start of the big change. What a smooth beginning.'

It is never a good idea to voice such sentiments. It is as though some malevolent force in the openings of the fabric of the universe is tuned in to such statements and then finds a way to wing itself down to cause as much mischief as possible.

The entrance examinations went very well. They were in English and Maths and Chiara was delighted to be able to do the long multiplication with ease and yes, she showed all her working. The English paper called for an essay and she managed to mention her helping out in the bookshop and her interest in operetta. Rosa also had topics which she was secure in writing about; they were less exciting than Chiara's array in scope, but she was skilled at expressing herself concisely and grammatically.

Dr Anderson, the head teacher, had been present at the examinations to welcome the girls.

The interviews were on different days, probably because the girls had surnames beginning with letters far apart in the alphabet. Lola and Pina accompanied Rosa, so that Lola could see the school too. Chiara was seen on a different day in the same week. When she got home that day, Rosa was waiting with Lola and Remo was preparing the tea.

When they sat down, Remo asked, 'So, what is this Dr Anderson like then?'

'Well,' said Rosa, 'she's not very tall. When she stood up from her desk to say hello to me she seemed rather short.'

'She's rather plump,' said Chiara, 'but that makes her look homely and the way she talked to me about my essay made me feel as if she was a cosy aunt like you read about in stories.'

'She smiled a lot,' said Rosa.

'Oh yes,' Chiara joined in, 'she was very smiley. I liked her a lot.'

'Me too,' said Rosa. 'She made me feel as if everything I said mattered.'

So the impressions of school and head teacher were both favourable in every respect and Pina sighed with relief. Another hurdle over.

- Four -

Then came the waiting for the next letter. It arrived, fortunately, on a school morning so Remo was waiting with it when Pina arrived home.

'Open it, then,' she said. 'Let's know the worst or the best.'

And there it was… the news… Chiara had a scholarship and a place at North London Collegiate…The best!

There was a second letter later in the morning: from the local authority; they would pay the fees but not the fares, as it was out of Borough and the parents could have chosen a more local school. But the fees would be paid.

Remo and Pina hugged each other tightly and Pina whispered, 'Well done, caro! But we can't tell Chiara yet.'

Remo frowned and thought for a moment.

'Of course,' he said, 'we need to know whether Lola has had her letter.'

'And what that says,' said Pina. 'If that news is not good, what do we do?'

They didn't have to wait long as unexpectedly there was a knock on the door early that same afternoon and there on the doorstep stood Lola, but with tears on her cheeks.

'Come in, cara,' said Pina. 'Remo, put the kettle on, please, it's Lola.'

Remo came to the kitchen door as Pina showed in her sister and sat her down. She withdrew her two letters from her pocket and Remo gently took one and Pina the other.

'But this is good news.' said Pina, reading the one from the school. 'Rosa has a place at the school, so why the tears?'

'Yes,' said Remo.' But not a scholarship and the local authority won't pay. This letter says Rosa has a place at Our Lady of Sion.'

'But,' rejoined Pina, 'North London says she has a place. Her exam scores were first rate and she interviewed well. So why won't Islington pay the fees?'

'I do not know,' said Remo, 'but the school letter asks us parents to make an appointment to see Dr Anderson as soon after receiving the letter as possible to discuss things.'

'I've already phoned the school,' said Lola, 'and I'll go the day after tomorrow. But it's no use. Rosa won't be able to go. There's no way that I can find that sort of money.'

'So where does that leave Chiara, then?' said Pina. 'Oh, of course, cara, you haven't heard. Chiara got in too. But she won't want to go without Rosa. Her heart's set on them going to school together. We'll have to let the school know that she won't be taking the place.'

'Let's just wait, a bit,' said Remo. 'Lola, say nothing at home yet. Let's speak to Chiara tonight and tell her what's happened. It will be hard for her. But she'll have to choose. Our Lady of Sion with Rosa, or North London Collegiate on her own. It's not a decision for us alone. And of course, there's no knowing if there are still places at Our Lady's. I didn't give a second or third choice.'

'What do you mean?' asked Lola, puzzled. 'Were there choices? In order of preference? I thought we just gave a list to the school. I wrote Our Lady and Sacred Heart at Hammersmith and North London. I was wondering why I had a letter from Our Lady's offering a place. I suppose it went down as the first choice. Maybe because Franca is already there. Oh no! What a mess. It's my fault.' And the tears welled up again.

'I'll come with you to Edgware,' said Remo, 'and we'll see what Dr Anderson has to say. Let's not despair at this stage. We can sort something out I am sure.'

And so with tea and this time truly proverbial sympathy, Lola was comforted and strengthened for the difficult times ahead.

- Five -

When Chiara came home from school with her father, she found the table set out in a special way.

'It's not my birthday,' she exclaimed, 'but there's cake!'

'Yes,' said Remo. 'And read the writing on it.'

'**Congratulations**,' she read. 'Congratulations?'

'You've passed,' said Pina. 'We had the letter this morning. So I made a quick lemon cake for tea to celebrate.'

'Really?' said Chiara. 'I've really passed? Oh thank you, Pina. Thank you, Pappa. And Rosa? Has she heard too?'

'Yes and no,' said Remo, hoping to deflect the conversation from taking the gloss of pleasure from Chiara's news.

'She has a place too,' said Pina. 'Like you, she's passed with full colours.'

'But…' said Chiara. 'There's a 'but' coming, I can feel it in the air.'

'There is,' said Remo.

'She can't take the place,' said Pina, 'because Lola would have to find the fees to pay for her.'

'Why?' asked Chiara.

And with some difficulty they tried to explain what might have happened.

'So, cara,' said Remo, 'this makes a difficult decision for you. School with Rosa at Sion or without Rosa at North London? You'll have to think about it carefully and then we'll do what is necessary.'

'Well, I don't see what the problem is,' said Chiara quite calmly. 'We can both go to North London. We've both passed.'

'But…' began Remo.

'No, wait. Think about this. You've often told me that my mamma left me money when she died. What was that for?'

'For you, cara,' said her father. 'For your future, your education, for what you might need. It was her legacy to you.'

'Exactly,' said Chiara. 'And have you needed to use any of it?'

'Not at all,' said Remo. 'We pay the convent fees from my earnings.'

'But if I hadn't won the scholarship, would you have used the money to send me to a private school again?'

'Well, yes, that's why I only put down one choice. I wanted you to go somewhere good, no matter what.'

'So, how about this? Use that money to pay Rosa's fees. There's enough isn't there? And she's as good as me.'

'No, I can't,' said Remo. 'Your mother left that for you.'

'For me, for my education, or for what I might need to make me happy? Could you see it that way?'

Remo looked at Pina. 'Well, I suppose so. I hadn't thought of it like that.'

'Well, Pappa, at the moment I'd like to share my happiness with Rosa. You know why, in a way.'

Pina looked puzzled and caught Remo's slight shake of the head, so said nothing.

'So if you both agree,' said Chiara, 'you can use the money for Rosa. I won't need it and I'll have her company to share all the excitements of the new school.'

Pina and Remo were silent.

'Let's have tea and cake,' said Pina and started to get things ready as Chiara opened her school bag and then went to wash her hands.

When they were all seated together, Remo spoke. 'We have to think carefully now,' he said. 'What do we tell Rosa? Obviously Lola would have to agree as well, but she's not telling Rosa anything, not even that she's passed, until she hears from us.'

'As it happens,' said Chiara, 'Miss Roche was doing proverbs with us today and we had this one: *What the eye doesn't see the heart doesn't grieve over.* And another one: *When ignorance is bliss, it's foolish to be wise* or something like that.'

'So are you saying,' said Pina, 'we should say nothing to Rosa?'

'Nothing at all. Ever! Imagine how she'd feel if she knew. And how might Franca feel, if *she* knew? It could spoil everything. Well, it would if it were me.'

'Chiara's right,' said Remo. 'Rosa mustn't know and perhaps when I see Dr Anderson with Lola we might be able to work something out for next year. Islington might reconsider, if we appeal and apply in a different year. Anyway, the money is not a problem. Are you sure about this, Chiara? That you don't want Rosa to know. Isn't it like there being a lie between you?'

'No, it won't be like that at all. Only the three of us know and Zia Lola will know. Everything will be fine. Believe me, I knew it would be when you took us there for the first time and I saw the cherubs peeping from the corners of the windows in the old house. Rosa saw them too and we both knew then.'

There was a pause.

'I'm waiting,' added Chiara. 'Patiently!'

And she sat upright and looked demure and smiled.

'Of course, cara,' said Pina offering her a knife as Remo slid the cake in front of her.

'Congratulations!' they both cried in unison as Chiara plunged the knife into the icing and measured out three more than healthy slices.

Fathers

Pina made it her priority to ask for an interview with Sister Angela once Chiara's place at North London Collegiate had been confirmed.

She was shown into the office and offered a seat.

'We would like to assure you, Sister, that although Chiara won't be going to a Catholic school in September, we've made arrangements with our parish priest for her to attend confirmation classes and she'll be confirmed in due course. We're tremendously grateful for your help in getting her into North London.'

'It was no trouble,' said Sister smiling as she heard the words that Pina offered.

'I did nothing but fill in the forms and send them off as requested.'

'I have a feeling,' said Pina, 'that it was not quite as simple as that. I feel sure that you must have added something. The letter we received was very enthusiastic about taking Chiara.'

'I may have written a little note,' said Sister ambiguously. 'I have met Dr Anderson in the past and she strikes me as a very caring woman. You were quite right, Mrs Romani, to find somewhere a little out of the ordinary for Chiara. She is a talented girl and needs to be encouraged and developed and the school you have chosen will certainly do that.'

'My husband and I are very grateful to you and the school for giving Chiara such a good start,' said Pina.

'Well, Miss Roche is the one to thank for that,' said Sister. 'We are blessed to have her with us. She is a treasure.'

Pina rose and extended her hand.

'Thank you again, Sister,' she said. 'I'm sure we shall be seeing you again before term ends.'

'I do hope so,' said Sister with a gleam returning to her eye. 'I do hope so.'

- Two -

When Pina returned home, she found Remo at the kitchen table with several letters in front of him and a totally bemused look on his face.

'I thought you were rushed off your feet with orders,' she said as she started to put the shopping away, noticing as she did so that the letter headings were all the same, from the American Embassy.

He shook his head. She stopped and looked more deliberately at the letters on the table.

'So, are we emigrating?' she asked. 'Give me good warning. Packing will be a big job and it will be a big journey for Chiara to do every day.'

Remo smiled. 'No, of course not,' he said. 'Come and sit down a moment, Pina. I need to talk to you and you may be rather cross with me.'

'And why would I be cross?' asked Pina curiously.

'Let me tell you how this has all come about,' Remo began.

'It started after you came back from the Christmas show *At the End of the Rainbow* or whatever. More trouble than it was worth, if you ask me. *Peter Pan* next year, for sure!'

Pina smiled. 'You're right. It was a bit heavy on sentimentality and I was aware that the girls weren't bubbling.'

'Far from it,' said Remo. 'Chiara told me that it had really upset Franca – all that business about finding lost family – as they hadn't heard from their father in ages. No cards, no parcels, nothing and her mother never wanted to talk about it, so she was upset. Chiara made me promise to try and find out what I could about their father.'

'Oh!' interrupted Pina.

'But she didn't want anyone else to know, not even you, in case there was bad news and things were worse than they are now. She thought you were bound to talk to Lola.'

'I see,' said Pina. 'Is this where I start to get cross?' she added, keeping a very straight face. 'I'm not sure,' said Remo glancing at her but not fixing his gaze on her.

'Well, carry on,' she said encouragingly.

'I've been in touch with the American Embassy, as you see, trying to trace Sergeant Frank DiMaggio. And today's letter has left me totally unsure what to do next. Things don't add up.'

'Well, they wouldn't,' said Pina. 'Carry on, caro, and explain what you've found out.'

'You know more than you're letting on,' said Remo, suddenly aware that his wife was being amazingly calm.

'Just carry on,' Pina replied.

'Well, at first they couldn't locate anyone by that name. Then they came up with an officer by that name. Then the bad news that he was missing in action presumed dead. That's this letter.' Remo shuffled through the papers and showed a letter to Pina.

'So I wrote again and told them he had a wife and daughters over here and asked if they were entitled to some sort of widow's compensation. There's the letter I had back today.' He passed over the most recent letter for Pina to read.

'I see,' she said. 'I understand why you're in a state.'

'But you don't seem surprised!' said Remo. 'You know all about this already, don't you?'

'Sisters don't keep secrets from each other,' said Pina. 'Of course I know what there is to know about this. Do you think Lola could have managed all this on her own?'

'Does she know then?' asked Remo. 'I mean, that she's not likely to get any kind of financial help from the army?'

'Of course,' replied Pina. 'How could she expect any, when Frank has a wife and son in Portland. They're the ones who are entitled, not her and the girls.'

'What?! He is married in the States as well? But Lola took his name. Were they married or not?'

They were married, yes, in a registry office. The marriage was later dissolved, I'm told, when he didn't return to this country. But she kept the name for the girls' sake.'

'But he must take responsibility for his children,' said Remo with passion.

'And it seems he did,' said Pina. 'For *his* child.'

'But, are you saying…?' said Remo.

'That the girls aren't his? Yes,' said Pina. 'I wish you'd talked to me first but there's no point in making a fuss about that now. This is how it is. I was in Italy, looking after my parents, as you know. Lola was in this country. She had a good job and was also involved with the war effort – lots of opportunities for girls to get stuck-in and learn new skills. She'd trained as a nurse and then during the early part of the war she went into various factories as a volunteer during her time off from nursing. Her main job kept her in military hospitals where they needed help. She had no ties in London so moved about. Sometime in 1941 she got involved with one of her patients who was brought back wounded. He was kept on service in this country and they fell in love and got married, as far as we know. He was a non-believer and you know what a palaver it is to get permission to marry a non-catholic so they just had a quiet ceremony at the local town hall wherever it was he was posted. We heard about all this in Italy by letter after the event and in that letter came news that Lola was pregnant and Franca was born in 1942. They lived in married quarters. Lola fell pregnant again and Rosa was born in 1943, the same year as Chiara. Then Frank, yes, he was Frank number one, was fit enough to be sent overseas again. He was part of the campaign at Monte Cassino, where he died. That was in 1944. So Lola was left a widow with two small children. She returned to London which of course was full of Americans at that time. It's not hard to understand how a still young woman was easily attracted to what American GIs had to offer. She fell for her second Frank. He took to the girls as well. It was easy for them to think of him as their father. He behaved that way, always visiting and sending stuff and there was certainly talk of Lola marrying him, and it happened, in a registry office. He was around a lot when he was stationed here. All home comforts. And I know that Lola changed her name to DiMaggio at the time. I think she liked the Italian connection and people easily accepted that being an Italian she would have an Italian husband. The girls have always used that surname.'

'So, do they not know about their real father?' asked Remo.

'Apparently not,' said Pina, 'but it's not as straightforward as that. When Lola changed her name, I asked about the girls' names on their birth certificates and she said there were no original certificates as she didn't register the births when they were born. This seemed very odd to me at the time. No public record of the births. One, I might have accepted, but both? I asked a bit more and got nowhere, she just clammed up. She eventually said that she registered both girls much later and put the father's name down as DiMaggio. I'm not even sure whether she was married to the first Frank or not, but look: it's done; it's over. If I scratch too much, I may ruin my relationship with her and she has no one else in this country. As far as I know, the girls are officially DiMaggio in the public records, and they believe they're daughters of an American in London during the war.'

'This leaves a lot of unanswered questions.' said Remo. 'A lot of *what if's* – the main one being a simple matter of mathematics.'

'How so?' said Pina.

'Well if Franca was born in '42 and the Americans only arrived that year…'

'Oh, I see,' said Pina. 'If they do ask questions…'

'And I know someone who'll be quick to spot that,' said Remo. 'It's a wonder she hasn't done so already, but I don't suppose she actually knows when the Yanks arrived here.'

'Yes indeed, caro,' replied Pina. 'Well, that's our problem. What do we tell Chiara? Or rather, what do you tell Chiara? I'm not supposed to know anything!' She smiled and put her hand on his shoulder.

He sighed.

'We'll think of something,' she said.

He turned his head and rested it against her.

'What would I do without you?' he said.

'You'd manage,' she replied, and then added, 'but not very well! And now, may I have another look at those letters?'

- Three -

When Chiara came down to breakfast a couple of days later, she looked worried.

'Pappa, have you noticed?' she said. 'I'm worried. The lamps in the street haven't been put out for days. I keep meaning to ask you if you've noticed.'

'That's odd,' said Remo. 'Our chap is so regular. You can set your clock by him. No, I hadn't noticed as the evenings are so light and so are the mornings.'

'I hope nothing's happened,' said Pina. 'Can you pop into the Town Hall and ask later?'

'I'll do that,' said Remo.

'I love watching the lamplighter,' said Chiara.

'It's so nice having a light that shines into my bedroom. He's been our lamplighter for a long time. When I was younger and went to bed earlier, I used to watch him knock the little bar with his long pole and wait to see the gas light up and he would always look up and wave or touch his cap, as if he was saying goodnight. I think he's quite old.'

'Not too old to ride a bike still,' said Pina. 'I've seen him on one. He leaves it at the end of the street and walks the length then collects it. Nice man.'

'Let's hope he's okay,' said Remo.

When he went to collect Chiara that afternoon, Remo was smiling.

'You did well to mention the lamplighter, cara. The office didn't know about the lamps not being seen to. Our man has retired. The new one is just learning the routes, which have been changed a bit. I think because he's younger they've added more streets. They were being kind to the old man! We're on the end of the old route which is why he always had his bike. The new one thought our street belonged to someone else. You would have thought he'd have known better. He's the son of our old lamplighter but clearly didn't listen to his old man's advice. Ah well, whoever listens to their old dad?' he added wryly. 'Still back to normal from tonight.'

Chiara thanked him and then said 'Pappa?'

'Yes, Chiara,' replied Remo, hoping that the conversation would not go down an avenue the end of which was not in sight.

'I want to ask you a question about fathers.'

His heart sank.

'Fathers? What sort of fathers? Holy fathers, priest fathers, fathers' fathers?'

'No, fathers and their day,' she added. I mean that special day fathers should have, like mothers.'

Remo sank back in relief.

'Yes, cara, but it's not an important day. I suppose they invented it because we have a mother's day and it was felt that dads deserved a special day too. In Italy it is always on St Joseph's day.'

'So what would you like?'

'Well the same as always in March when it comes around... we celebrate Pina's saint's day and the day for dads, so we'll treat it the same as usual. Probably on the nearest Sunday. Just an ordinary Sunday is fine. Every Sunday is special anyway even during these difficult times. Pina has always managed somehow to make Sunday special with what she cooks. However I do have news that might make it easier for such a day to be special in future.'

'Oh?'

'News to please you too.'

'What's that?'

'Rationing is ending. No more ration books. So more of everything.'

'Including sweets?'

'I imagine so.'

'So can we get some peppermint creams from Lyons for Pina?'

'Tomorrow, cara. A great idea.'

- Four -

When they reached home, the first question Chiara had for Pina was: 'Was Mrs Morgan in it today, Pina? I'm sure she was in the Radio Times this week.'

'No, cara,' Pina replied, 'but you'll never guess what Sally's up to this week.'

'You mean *Selly*,' said Remo. 'I never understand why they can't call her Sally. I'll leave you two to gossip. A cup of tea would be nice when you've finished discussing *The Diary*!'

Chiara loved *Mrs Dale's Diary* but she never got to listen to it during a school week, only in the holidays or on the rare occasions when she wasn't well and stayed home from school. So she used to keep her finger on the pulse of what was happening in Park Wood Hill by reading the synopsis in Radio Times and the cast list and then quizzing Pina, who built her morning or afternoon around the broadcast or its repeat. They treated the characters as if they were real and discussed their daily doings regularly and animatedly much to Remo's dismay. Their *Diary* time was his cue to make off to do his paper work, but the doors were open and bits of plot-line tended to drift through and into his subconscious. Today was no different.

'You know Bob went off to Wales when he heard Jenny intended to give up her job,' continued Pina.

'I thought he managed to persuade her to return to London with him,' said Chiara, hoping rather for details of what Mrs Morgan was up to, or even what Monument was doing in the garden or where Captain was. The slushy romantic love story lines had little appeal to her at this age.

'He did,' said Pina who liked these storylines the best, 'but you remember Jenny's father?'

'Yes,' said Chiara, 'he's a bit of a misery. Good job all fathers aren't like him,' she added more loudly, suppressing a laugh and pointing towards the open door to Remo's study.

The laughter attracted Remo's attention and he listened in a bit more carefully to the involved and complicated plot.

'Well,' continued Pina, 'he's refused to let Bob and Jenny get engaged. I think it's because he doesn't want Jenny to be too far from home now that her mother's unwell. But he's just being selfish. But he can stop them as Jenny is underage.'

Remo realised why he had little time for these endless ramifications in relationships and was suddenly quite disturbed and then determined.

'So, what's happened with Angela Wade?' asked Chiara. 'I thought she was in love with Bob.'

'Oh, she still is, but her father won't tell her that Bob's not in love with her. He's afraid of what effect that might have on her just as she's started to walk again after the accident.'

'So where does Selly figure in all this?' asked Chiara.

'Ah well, Jenny has asked Sally to tell her nephew that she is going to give up her career on the stage after all and will be going back to Wales to look after her mother. Poor old Sally, what a job!'

'What do you think will happen?' said Chiara.

'Nothing, for a very long time,' said Pina. 'No happy ending in sight at all. I think Jenny suspects that Bob's in love with Angela and wants to leave him free.'

No happy ending in sight. These words struck home for Remo and he knew what he had to do.

'Is there any chance of that tea?' he called out. 'I can be a grumpy miserable old father too when I want. And if I am provoked too far.'

And Chiara hurried to pour out his cup and take it along to him.

- Five -

The weather was very unsettled. The months of summer that everyone had been looking forward to were overshadowed by rain clouds. Everyone hoped they would clear before the school holidays started but the showers were relentless and Chiara adopted a new song that she heard on the radio and unconsciously set about driving her family quietly mad by singing it whenever it started to rain.

'*If I had a golden umbrella, with the sunshine on the inside and a rainbow on the outside, what a wonderful day it would be.*' It was relentlessly jolly and rather repetitive so that once the tune was begun, it just went round and round in your mind. And because it was so cheerful about taking people under your umbrella and making them happy, there was a point usually at which you wanted to throw something at the singer, especially if you weren't feeling so cheerful yourself.

'It makes no sense,' said Remo, 'A rainbow on the outside. Are you sure it's not saying rainfall on the outside? That would at least be realistic.'

'Yes but not so lovely,' said Chiara, 'so I sing rainbow, not rainfall… la la la, la la la, la la la!'

'Please, cara, give it a rest!' exclaimed Remo, frustrated. But he realised his frustration was caused by his inability to deal with the issue of the American Embassy. Pina had told him to leave things with her. But nothing was happening. Father's day had come and gone, and whenever fathers were mentioned, a cold shudder passed through him. He had all but given up hope of dealing with the situation when one evening after supper, while all three were around the table, Pina spoke up.

'I know all about your little conspiracy,' she began. Chiara looked puzzled. Remo stiffened. 'Your father promised to keep it between the two of you, I know,' said Pina, 'but it wasn't possible, cara. I saw the letter and had to ask him and he couldn't refuse to tell me. After all Lola is my sister. But you're not to worry. I've not said a word to her, and what we do about the news will be up to you as you started this ball rolling.'

She put her hand into the pocket of her apron and produced just one envelope.

Chiara could see that it was from the American Embassy and she noted the heading on the top of the letter that was taken out. Pina unfolded the paper carefully and read out the details, but substituted the surname of DiMaggio for the one typed in the letter.

'So their father is dead,' Chiara said. '*Missing in action*, you said. That means he's probably dead, doesn't it?'

'I'm afraid so, cara,' said Remo, realising that from all of the correspondence and from his conversation with Pina, just this one simple piece of evidence was going to be allowed. He took the letter from Pina's hands and ,after scanning it himself as if it was new to him, quietly pushed it to one side, intending to dispose of it as soon as possible now that it had served its purpose.

'So, cara,' he said, 'the question is, do you tell the girls or not?'

'Surely Zia Lola knows this already?' said Chiara.

'Yes, she does,' replied Pina.

'But she's chosen not to tell Franca and Rosa.'

'That's right.'

'But why? Shouldn't they know?'

'Perhaps, but not at this point in their lives,' said Pina.

'But if he died fighting, then he was a hero and...'

'But we don't know that,' said Remo. 'The letter says *missing in action* so he might one day return, but the chances are very slim when an authority writes like that.'

'So Zia Lola must have her reasons why she doesn't tell the girls and won't talk about it to them. I can only imagine what those reasons might be,' said Pina, cautiously, avoiding a deliberate lie.

'Well,' said Chiara, 'if their mother chooses not to tell them, it's not really up to me to do so either, is it?'

'I tend to agree with you,' said Remo.

'Perhaps Zia will talk to them when they're older,' said Chiara. 'I don't think they should know now. It won't do them any good. It's not going to make any difference to the way they live, unless people ask them about their dad. Franca's new friends at school didn't ask anything but perhaps Rosa's will at our new school. What could she say? She can't say nothing and seem stupid.'

'The easiest thing to say is that he died in the war,' said Pina. 'Many children lost parents that way. He was in the services and he died. Not many people would ask much more. It was quite a common occurrence.'

'I think someone should tell them that's what they should say,' said Chiara.

'Well maybe you can do that when they seem to need that sort of help,' said Remo. 'If you like. you could tell them then that I did write away and I had that reply. But tell them as well not to bring it up with their mother unless she talks about it first. She's clearly too deeply upset by it to make it a topic with them. Let them consider her feelings.'

'But,' added Pina, 'I suggest you don't raise the subject unless one of the girls does first, and maybe only bring it up with Rosa when you start your new school.'

'That's a really good idea, Pina. Thank you both.'

'Time for bed in a while,' said Remo.

'Oh, can I stay up a bit later? Please?'

'Why? Oh, don't tell me. It's *Hello Playmates* night! And we have to sit through Arthur Askey and his buzzy bee songs. I think I prefer your umbrella!'

'It's not him, I like,' said Chiara. 'It's Mrs Purvess and her daughter Nola.'

'Silly custard!' exclaimed Pina, and both laughed.

'Oh, I see I'm outnumbered again,' said Remo. 'Yes alright. Get yourself ready and then come down when it's on.' Chiara said her thanks and left quickly to find a book for half an hour of quiet reading.

- Six -

Remo looked at Pina and smiled.

'Thank you,' he said. 'A simple solution but probably effective.'

'I hope so,' said Pina. 'Now, don't do something like that again, please. If it's family matters, talk to me. You and your daughter! What a pair! She's obviously inherited something in her nature from you or her mother!'

'Or perhaps she's developed something from being brought up by you as her mother,' added Remo. 'What do they say? Nature or Nurture?'

'No,' said Pina, 'she's clearly inherited your first wife's characteristics.'

'Well, I would have to agree with you there,' said Remo. 'As you're now agreeing with me.'

Pina looked puzzled.

'What are you saying now?' she said.

'I am agreeing that she's developed my first wife's characteristics, my dear. You see, you're my first wife and the only wife I've ever had.'

Mothers

'Pappa, I need you,' Chiara's voice travelled from the sitting room through to the kitchen. 'I can't tune the wireless properly. It's starting soon.'

Remo was just sitting with a calm smile on his face. Pina had a rather blank expression and a slightly furrowed forehead.

'You'd better go,' she said. 'We don't want to keep Mrs Purvess waiting. And you won't want to miss a minute of Arthur Askey!'

'Ha ha,' said Remo, rising. 'Silly custard!'

And, followed by Pina, he left for the sitting room where Chiara was already ensconced in her corner of the sofa, clutching a cushion. She patted the seat and when Pina sat down, she tucked the cushion behind her back. Remo twiddled to correct the wavelengths until they gave a clear reception. As he took to the armchair he laid his hand on Pina's head briefly, but reassuringly. And so the familiar signature tune started and Arthur Askey's jovial greeting '*Hello Playmates*' set them off into a half an hour of silliness and laughter.

As the closing music faded, Remo switched off the set and Chiara jumped up.

'Thank you both,' she said.

'Off to bed now, cara. And no reading tonight. School tomorrow.'

'Yes. Night, night, Pina.' And she kissed her on both cheeks. 'Night, night, Pappa. Don't forget to turn out the lamplight tonight, will you!'

'Off with you,' they both said, 'Silly custard!'

Two

They waited until they heard the bedroom door close upstairs. Then Remo closed the sitting room door and came and sat back in the armchair, opposite Pina.

'Why now?' she asked. 'Why after all this time have you decided to break this news now?'

'It feels right,' said Remo. 'When you said about the Lola business that it shouldn't happen again – us not talking about family things – it brought it home to me that there are matters that you really should know about.'

'So you and Chiara's mother were never married?'

'That's right,' said Remo.

'I knew a little about things before I came to work here for you,' said Pina, 'as Fr Martyn gave me some help in making my decision.'

'He's a good man,' said Remo, 'and knows a lot about my background but not everything. No one knows everything except me. And soon you will as well. I hope it won't be hard for you.'

'I don't like the word *illegitimate*,' said Pina 'but you're telling me that Chiara might be called that, because you weren't married to her mother. But why? Why didn't you marry her, especially when you knew she was pregnant?'

'I couldn't. Even if I'd wanted to.' said Remo. 'Mariella, Chiara's mother was my sister.'

Pina's eyes grew wide. 'So you're not…you are Chiara's…uncle. The uncle that the letter spoke about who would…How? Why?'

'Stay calm, cara, and I'll tell you all I can as simply as possible.'

'I'm a bit stunned,' said Pina, 'but I'm beginning to see straight again and maybe understand a little.'

'Mariella and I were still quite young when our parents died. We inherited their house in the village and some land. I'd done my training in art and even while my father was still alive I had converted part of the house into a workshop and had installed a kiln. Mariella was a little older than me and looked after all of us after our mother died. Then my father died too. The war came. I was called up. We had leased out the farm land to neighbours once it was clear that I wouldn't be a farmer, so there was an income from the fields, partly in money and partly in produce. My father had married into quite a wealthy family and my mother had brought a considerable dowry to the marriage, mainly in jewellery and gold which fortunately we stashed away. Mussolini's movement was whipping up tremendous support, with women – even married women in England – sending their wedding rings to finance the war effort. We put some of the money in the bank in Bologna but some we just took and buried for safe keeping under the outhouses of the family home. It sounds foolish, I know, but we were terrified there would be confiscations.

'Mariella inherited this of course. She'd sold some of the jewels to equip my studio when I decided to come back and live and work in the village.

'When I was called up, the village was virtually deserted; just a few old men were left, and the women. Like many another village, they weren't left in peace. Few villages were left undisturbed. There were soldiers everywhere: mostly our own men going north to the Alps on Mussolini's orders to secure the borders with France. Soldiers don't always respect what's on their journey to their death.

'Mariella was caught unawares. She was treated savagely, brutally, according to neighbours who found her. It was the same with other young women in the village. No one was spared. The soldiers ransacked the house for anything of value but of course failed to find anything much except my statuettes. Plaster and wooden saints are not much use on a campaign. Maybe it was that frustration of finding nothing of value that made them behave so cruelly. The shock of the attack totally wrecked my sister, but she became even worse when she discovered she was pregnant. She was taken to a convent and it was the sisters there who managed to contact me with the news. I was given leave and went to find my sister. She was even then a mere shadow of herself, incoherent and distraught. She had periods of clarity and calm but it was obvious to me and to the sisters that she couldn't return to the family home and fend for herself and a child. She totally rejected the child, as if by doing so, the whole business of her rape and pregnancy would disappear. Her mental state was never restored for any length of time.

'The birth had to be registered. With the connivance of the Mother Superior, we entered my name as that of the father on the documents and we put down that the mother had died giving birth. The authorities made no enquiries. The nuns took care of both mother and child. I promised I would make good their expenses as soon as I could.

'When the war ended, my service came to an end as well. I returned to the farm and packed up as much as I could. Then through agents, I put the house and land on the market. My neighbours were only too pleased to buy the land and they had a son returning from the army as well who was in need of separate housing. I retrieved the jewellery of course. Their sale more than compensated the sisters for their kindness and made it possible for Mariella to be transferred to a sanatorium where she lived out the rest of her troubled life.

'I always tried to go and visit her there when I had work to do in Italy. She rarely recognised me but it was on one of those rare occasions that she spoke to me of Chiara and gave me the letter and the package of felt animals that she had made. The sisters had constantly tried to bring her mind round to thinking about her daughter and had saved the animals she had painstakingly made. I didn't know what to do with them. I couldn't destroy them because they were the only connection that Chiara could have with her mother, but I didn't know how to present them to her as her mother was always presumed dead.

'You know how long it has taken me to try and find a way of handing them over to her. If I delayed much longer Chiara would have grown out of finding them attractive. She's still young enough to love soft toys.

'The letter was more difficult to deal with: it's the only piece of writing from Mariella to her daughter. I knew the contents but I couldn't bring myself to destroy it.

'I contrived the arrival of the parcel. The stamps were easy to assemble over time but the paper wasn't totally convincing. I arranged with the neighbours to make that unexpected delivery which passed over quite convincingly, I think.

'I knew way back then that I couldn't bring Chiara up in Italy. It was too close to her mother's situation for the child to grow up without being affected by it. I had contacts in London and knew there'd be a market for my statuettes here, if not for my wood carving. I negotiated the purchase of this house and business and then collected Chiara who was nearly three by then and was being looked after by nuns, not her mother. Armed with my paperwork that designated her as my daughter, I arranged for as much as I could to be shipped to London and we arrived to live here. Chiara's inheritance – the money for her education – is of course, the gold and other items that are lodged in the bank. I can explain those details in due course.

'So there you have it. Now the question will be: do I or don't I? Should Chiara know or not? But first, once you've taken all this in, just ask anything that concerns you. Now that I've opened the door, there are no more secrets.'

Pina sat back.

'Yes,' she said. 'I do have questions and my first is: how long do I have to wait before you make me a cup of coffee?'

Remo relaxed.

'Black, perhaps, and I think, just a little grappa to go with it.'

'Sounds good to me,' said Pina and sank back into the sofa, thinking.

- Three -

When Remo returned with the tray of coffee and two glasses, generously filled, he set them down and then sat down next to Pina on the sofa.

'So what do you make of this then?' he asked.

'I am…overwhelmed…' Pina replied, '…with such love for you that I can't begin to put it into words. When I lived in Italy with my parents, I never dared to hope I'd ever have a family of my own. I longed for the chance to make a home for someone else, especially after my parents died. And then this opportunity to come and work for you and Chiara happened and led to our marriage. But there was always a shadow over our marriage – the shadow of your first wife. I've always felt I might not be good enough – not because of the way you've behaved towards me, but because of the way I am – anxious that I was second-best, in a way. And today that shadow has disappeared. Of all the women in the world, you waited and chose me, only me, to share your home, your life, your daughter.

'Oh yes, there's no doubt, caro. Chiara is your daughter. No amount of papers, documents, certificates, forms could ever make it otherwise. Nor will they if, as you say, you've done everything in proper order.'

'I have,' said Remo. 'Let me tell you a little more after a sip of coffee.'

They settled on the sofa next to each other and Remo continued. 'The thing that worried me most, when I was planning how to make Chiara's life as carefree as possible in the future, was how to cover tracks that would lead her to unhappiness. What if she started questions about her mother's grave? What if she wanted to know about her family tree? Her grandparents? So many *what ifs*. I've often felt defeated when I start to think about such things.'

'Can we ever cover up truth entirely?' asked Pina. 'I don't think so. But there's a time when finding out the truth can be less hurtful and harmful, and I agree with you that for Chiara that time is not now. So tell me what you have arranged and at least we'll be able to support each other in protecting her.'

So Remo settled down to elaborate on all sorts of details.

'I could never have managed without the nuns' help,' he said. 'I don't know why they're so often regarded as figures of fun, or as cruel and manipulative. Both here and in Italy, there's a feeling of hostility towards them, but they've seen me through all my difficulties which is why I wanted Chiara to be taught by them at the start.'

'You chose well with the convent,' said Pina. 'They are excellent there and they have dear Miss Roche as well. Chiara will miss them when she transfers.'

'But before that happens,' said Remo, 'we have a trip to Italy to fix up.'

'We're staying at my parents' house then?' asked Pina. 'As agreed?'

'Of course,' Remo replied. 'I thought Lola was bringing the girls too.'

'Yes, but she cannot stay as long as we can, as she has limited holiday from work.' said Pina. 'So she'll take the girls over and they can come back with us if they want, or return with her. Whatever works out best.'

'I want to take Chiara to my parents' part of the country for a few days,' said Remo. 'It might allay questions if she sees something of her roots, her background.'

'But your old home has gone, hasn't it?' asked Pina.

'Well it's totally altered. There are new owners now. They've used the shell of the building and built onto it so it's unrecognisable. There's no one left in the village from my parents' time, nor from when we grew up there as children. The younger generation all moved away. The older ones who had some knowledge of what happened to my sister have all died. So, no one to answer any questions or remember me.

'I've seen to a memorial stone in the cemetery. It already had the names of my parents on it, and in the space underneath I had inscribed:

con
carissima Mariella
fratello con sorella
uniti

'No dates?' asked Pina. 'And why mention the brother?'

'No dates, no questions, no answers,' replied Remo.

'If I'm asked then I shall say Mariella had no family of her own except her brother. They were orphaned (which is stretching the truth but is not a lie). So she lies there with my parents.'

'And the brother? That's you!'

'Well, what to do with the box of animals and that letter threw me for quite a while. But then I decided it was best to acknowledge the uncle somehow. He disappeared during the war. We may assume he dies somewhere and that he's now united with his sister. Neither too much, nor too little, I hope.'

'And his name?' asked Pina.

'Well, I think he has to have the same first name as me. A curious coincidence perhaps, but the name is not uncommon.'

'It should be enough,' said Pina, 'especially in the light of Franca's situation and the way that *missing in action* has to be enough to satisfy the girls. As to the future...'

'That has to take care of itself,' said Remo. 'You have no idea what a relief it is to have this in the open at last.'

'I can understand that,' said Pina, nestling closer and reaching for her glass of grappa.

- Four -

A couple of days after the end of term, Remo made his way on his own back to the convent school, a journey he had made almost daily for the last six years. It was an odd feeling to think that this walk to Duncan Terrace would be perhaps the last he would make so he was pleased that his purpose was a sound one.

He asked to see Sister Angela. He knew that she would have to be there tidying away the end of a school year and preparing for a new September.

He was shown into her office and offered a seat. She was not there and when she did arrive she was clearly flustered. She was wearing an apron over her habit and her face showed some anxiety. She quickly removed the apron as if to re-establish the role she needed to take for the occasion.

'Don't get up, Mr Romani,' she said with a wave of the hand as she made her way to the desk. 'To what do I owe this pleasure?'

Remo had risen fully and waited for her to be seated before he resumed his seat.

'Thank you for seeing me without an appointment, Sister,' he began.

'I hope nothing has gone wrong with the transfer,' she said anxiously.

'Be assured, sister. All is well. I've come merely to express our thanks for what you've done for Chiara during her time here and especially in these last weeks.'

'Nothing more than my duty,' said the nun, glancing down at her desk.

'Oh I think you've gone beyond duty,' said Remo.

'Well, perhaps it is when we go beyond what is imposed on us that we truly gain pleasure in our work,' the nun replied. 'Duty is what is expected of us, but going a step further and achieving something worthwhile is truly satisfying.'

'Well it's to thank you for that extra step that I've come today,' said Remo, 'and to offer you this little token of our gratitude. I believe you did at one time hope for a statue for the school.'

He produced a box from under his chair and set it on the desk.

'I know this is not quite what you were expecting but then it's not for the school. It's for you personally.'

'May I open it now?' asked the nun curiously.

'Yes, please do,' said Remo. 'I may have to apologise for it.'

'Now I am curious,' replied the nun as she removed the lid. The sides of the box fell down as the lid was taken off and the statuette stood swathed in tissue paper which she proceeded to unwrap.

There before her stood a wooden carving of a nun. Dressed in the full habit of the sisters of the cross and passion, it had its back to Sister Angela. She turned it round to face her and gave a slight gasp. The figure was depicted with its arms open. Under its right arm was a carving of a small boy, under its left that of a small girl, both in full school uniform. The hands of the figure of the nun rested on their shoulders. The nun was shown smiling and wearing a pair of small round glasses.

'I started by thinking that I would make a statuette of your namesake, the angel, Angela,' said Remo, 'but then I thought what an impression the picture in the first class has always made on Chiara. The picture of the guardian angel. So I changed my plan a little to combine ideas. I hope you're not offended,' he added, as there was a rather stunned silence from the other side of the desk.

'Not at all, Mr Romani. Not at all. I'm lost for words.'

'Well, I thought that when you finally retire from your school work, it might be a nice reminder of your days here and your vocation, to guard and protect and guide our children.'

The nun was now bustling with one hand under her habit to produce a small handkerchief into which she blew gently and with which she dabbed her cheek, masking her face for a moment while she composed herself.

'This is more than generous, Mr Romani.'

'Oh, by the way, I asked our parish priest to bless it for you,' Remo added, 'to save you any embarrassment.'

'Thank you so much,' replied the nun as Remo got to his feet. 'I shall miss Chiara but remember you in my prayers, and especially whenever I catch sight of my little award.'

She rose and extended her hand to Remo who touched it lightly, gave a slight bow and with a smile left the nun to enjoy her statuette.

- Five -

A few days later the family was off from Victoria on the boat train to catch the ferry across the channel. They were bound for Italy, escaping the greyness of England and looking forward to the sunshine of their other home.

Their arrival in the village was met with great delight not just by Lola and the girls but by the other villagers who were always pleased to have Pina back among them.

Almost the first question Pina had to answer was whether she would rejoin the church cleaning rota while she was there in the summer. To which of course she always agreed.

The holiday settled into an easy pattern. For a while Remo absented himself to revisit old friends and business associates in the other parts of the North, and on one of these occasions he took Chiara with him. Pina was on tenterhooks during these few days as she knew that he would be taking Chiara to see the area where he had lived and to show her the gravestone in the cemetery. But on their return, all seemed to have passed without incident. Chiara in her matter of fact way described her visit and shared with everyone at supper the scant details she had been given about her uncle who had gone missing during the war. Because of the resonances with their own situation, the girls made little comment and Lola stayed very quiet.

It came as a surprise then when Lola's time to return to London arrived some three weeks into the holiday that Chiara asked if she might return with the girls and Lola and stay with them rather than stay in the village and return with Remo and Pina, about a week later.

Pina saw it as a good sign of Chiara showing some independence and of making her new life blend in more with that of Rosa. When she asked how Lola felt about it, her sister smiled. She was only too pleased to give Remo and Pina some time on their own, for the first time ever, and had no problem in taking Chiara back. In fact it solved a problem of what Rosa would do while Lola was back at work. She would have company.

And so, once they had all packed up and been safely seen onto the *corriere* and waved off, Remo and Pina walked slowly back up to the house together.

It felt very quiet after the hustle and bustle of four other people. Pina made a simple supper for that evening: a risotto with mushrooms and a salad of characteristic cultivated dandelion leaves, chicory and tomatoes, all gifts from the neighbours who grew far too much for their own use.

Remo opened a bottle of wine made by one of the men in the village from grapes on Pina's land. It was a red wine but with a sparkle, and they enjoyed their meal sitting outside and facing the setting sun. It was peaceful and neither felt the need to speak. To be in each other's company was sufficient. Each sat with particular thoughts and automatically stretched out their hands across the table and closed their eyes, letting the sun warm their faces while the house martins wheeled and danced their evening passegiata through the darkening sky.

- Six -

The following day, Remo had business in a neighbouring village with a priest who needed advice on the wooden Calvary outside his church. Remo had hired a car for the holiday so they would be mobile for outings. He asked Pina if she would like to accompany him but she had written herself into the cleaning rota for that day and so decided not to go.

As she fell back into the familiar pattern of cleaning and polishing which came as second nature to her in this church, with its beams and pews and its meaningful carvings of the saints, she suddenly felt herself back all those years ago and recalled the emptiness of those days and the fullness of her present life. She went to the statue of the Madonna and child and pulled out her kneeling pad, and before she settled into prayer she took from her pocket a long narrow envelope and placed it carefully between the outstretched hands of the child in the Madonna's arms. On the front of the envelope was written simply *Padre Girolamo*.

After she had put it in place, she settled into her familiar cycle of prayers, gazing as she spoke them into the faces of both mother and child.

Their evenings on their own that week soon followed a pattern. They would take their simple supper onto the terrace at the back of the house from which there was a view down to the river, unspoiled by any sort of building. The house was at the top end of the village and so slightly away from neighbours which is why they knew that they would not be disturbing anybody if they brought out the wind-up gramophone. Pina's parents had accumulated a stock of records, mainly operatic and many folksongs and popular ballads. Their favourite singer had been Gigli and their love for him had been inherited by both Pina and Lola who would always try to go to a concert at the Albert Hall when he was performing. Pina and Remo were working their way through the collection of records and Remo kept returning to:

Non Ti Scordar Di Me – 'Do Not Forget Me'

As they settled down again for the evening with their wine and the gramophone, Pina nestled into Remo's side on the garden couch.

They listened again to the record and then she said, 'I'm sure I've guessed why you love that record so much!'

'Oh yes? And why might that be?'

'Because you're missing Chiara,' said Pina. 'The song is about swallows leaving, and the singer is asking his own little swallow not to forget him. And saying that there's always a nest for her in his heart. Remo, you're blushing,' exclaimed Pina.

'Weeell, I do miss her,' admitted Remo, 'but that's something we're going to have to adjust to. And it's wonderful to have this time to ourselves.'

'I was looking today as I cleaned the statues,' said Pina, 'and was struck again by how well you captured Chiara's expression when you carved the divine child.'

'Chiara's features?' asked Remo puzzled. 'No, I made that statue long before Chiara was born. Those features were Mariella's when she was a child. My parents had old photographs and I remember using one for the infant and another from when Mariella was a young woman for the face of the Madonna.'

'So they are both Mariella?' said Pina.

'Yes,' replied Remo. 'I've never had the chance to use an infant for the model of a baby Jesus.'

The record had stopped playing and Pina rose, shuffled among the other records until she found what she wanted. She put it on and cranked the handle of the machine. It was Gigli singing the Tosti song *Aprile*.

She said nothing as she settled back and took Remo's hand.

'Well, caro, you'll never be able to say that again.'

He turned towards her and saw her face radiant in the light of the evening sun. She nodded in answer to his unasked question.

She put her finger on his lips and indicated that they should let Gigli have the last word.

é l'April'! é l'April'!

Then the last B flat floated out into the evening air and Remo took Pina into his arms.

é l'April'!

Suggestion

As far as I know, at the time of printing, all the tunes, songs and music mentioned in the text are available to enjoy on YouTube. Episodes of the radio programmes too can be found, even the opening harp music for Mrs Dale's Diary. It would be particularly good if, as a reader, you were able to listen to the Gigli songs that conclude the story.

Appreciation

I would like to thank my artist friend Doug for his work on the cover. His skills have brought this volume in line with the earlier two books that Holywell has printed.

I am grateful for all the help and patience that Holywell has given me during this project and am particularly pleased that Toby Matthews once again has seen it through to completion.

I am grateful to Denise (Harfitt) Reynolds and Gilda (Zazzi) Reeves for their recollections of going to school in Duncan Terrace, not quite at the same time as Chiara, but close enough.

I would like to thank Joan Lundy for meeting me for a very enjoyable afternoon tea full of reminiscences about the proceedings for examinations in the fifties at North London Collegiate School. The School has remained a piece of paradise in London for the education of girls.

I am grateful to my friend Andrea Chappell for allowing me to borrow some of her sunflowers. One of the stumbling blocks for me with this book has been trying to find appropriate illustrations: nothing seemed to fit the bill so I have opted for bursts of brightness that do in fact mirror the text in some ways without actually illustrating it.

The frontispiece is a water colour by another dear friend, Audrey Willis, who can no longer wield a brush. Its inclusion here is a thank-you to her for the many works of art she created for me over the years.

As I have said elsewhere, the fictional characters interact with people who really did exist but whose conversations and behaviour are totally fictionalised. I hope I have not served anyone poorly.

Last, but far from least, I wish to record my never-failing love and appreciation of my father and my mother for giving me a wonderful childhood, in Finsbury, once upon a time.